ORPHEUS

Modern Middle East
Literatures in Translation Series

ORPHEUS

Nazli Eray

Translated from the Turkish by
Robert Finn

Introduction by
Sibel Erol

The Center for Middle Eastern Studies
The University of Texas at Austin

Cover design: Diane Watts
Series editor: Jeanette Herman

Library of Congress Control Number: 2006928457
ISBN 978-0-292-71409-0

The publication of this book was supported in part by a grant
from the Turkish Ministry of Culture and Tourism.

ACKNOWLEDGEMENTS

I would like to thank Nazli Eray for her help in translating her work; Sibel Erol's students at New York University, Kristin Dickinson, Vanessa H. Larson, and Mackensey Bauman, who made many valuable suggestions regarding the translation and correlating different editions of the work; and Amy Dowling Kear, who inspired me to undertake the task of rendering Orpheus into English. I would also like to thank Helena and Edward Finn, for accompanying me on the long trip to the Underworld of Translation.

-Robert Finn

CONTENTS

INTRODUCTION
Sibel Erol

Nazli Eray is one of the most beloved and prolific storytellers
of contemporary Turkish literature. Born in 1945 in Istanbul, Eray
graduated from Arnavutkoy Kiz Lisesi[1] then studied law and philosophy
at Istanbul University before she dropped out and moved to Ankara
to work as a translator for the Ministry of Tourism. After she married
and gave birth to twin daughters, she quit her job and devoted herself
to writing. Eray has published 25 books since her professional debut in
1967 with her collection *Ah Bayim Ah* (Ah, Mister, Ah). Most of her books
are short story collections, but she has also written plays like *Erostratus*
(1985)[2] and novels, like her latest book, *Beyoglunda Gezersin* (You Wander
Through Beyoglu, 2005). Eray's writing has been recognized in Turkey
by prestigious awards such as *The Haldun Taner Short Story Prize*, given
to her collection *Yoldan Gecen Oykuler* (Stories Passing By the Road) in
1988, and the *Yunus Nadi Prize for the Novel*, awarded to *Ask Giyinen
Adam* (The Man Who Wears Love) in 2002. Her stories "Monte Kristo,"
"Underdevelopment Pharmacy," and "The Cellular Engineer" have been
published in English translation,[3] and a collection of her stories appeared
in German in 1986.

Orpheus, originally published in 1983, retells the popular myth
from the perspective of a modern Eurydice, searching for Orpheus in a
Turkish coastal town on the Mediterranean, whose rapid urbanization
is literalized through the arrival of the capital city, Ankara, figured as
an actual person. The novella begins when Eurydice arrives in the town
and arranges to meet an enigmatic assistant who calls himself Mr. Night.
They go every night to a house they identify as belonging to Orpheus,
watching it from 400 meters away. On one of these nights, they happen

upon a statue of the second-century Roman emperor Hadrian, half-buried in an archaeological dig. Communicating through letters carried by a pigeon, the statue and Eurydice begin a correspondence, in the course of which Eurydice agrees to show Hadrian the Bertolucci film *Last Tango in Paris*, which to her mind embodies the ethos of modern life. The novel ends at dawn the night they show the film to Hadrian. As the last scene is projected onto Orpheus' house, he comes out to the balcony and becomes part of the murder scene taking place.[4]

In its plot line, *Orpheus* is a simple story made up of repetitions, and this sense of simplicity is further reinforced by Eray's stylistic use of the rhythms and vocabulary of everyday conversational language. Here, as in the rest of her oeuvre, language is a transparent, unproblematic means of communication. However, the air of simplicity this lends the work is entirely misleading, because, in essence, this is a foil to the text's web of nebulous allusions lurking suggestively beneath its surface, and to the chaos of surreal events floating above it. Eray's use of the fantastic allows her work to function at all of these levels, which are thematized and literalized as the earth, the underground, and the air in *Orpheus*. Eray connects these three levels through a collage of intertextual references and suggestive details that refuse the logic of cause and effect, that coexist not as thresholds of intelligibility guiding readers through a linear progression, but rather as spiraling variations on the same theme, accessible through multiple points of entry. Readers thus will see in Eray's work what they are ready to see, whether they enjoy the humorous events on the surface or delve deeper into the intertextual allusions for a richer understanding. The misleading simplicity of her language and the democratic accessibility of her style have led Eray to be viewed more as a popular author than a literary one. She is clearly both.

Eray and the Fantastic

Without exception, all of Eray's works are written in the fantastic mode, consciously engaging with the idea of a new reality that functions as a critique of the status quo.[5] I use the term "fantastic" as Todorov defines it, as the genre that frustrates the resolution of whether or not a supernatural story is true.[6] He explains that even if the character is still disoriented and thus unable to decide, the reader must decide by the end of the narrative whether there is a natural explanation for its supernatural events. If s/he decides there is indeed a realist explanation, then the narrative ends in the *uncanny*. If realist explanations are inadequate to account for the events, the narrative ends in the *marvelous*, signaling a new reality. According to Todorov, the fantastic is a temporary and transitional genre that must resolve itself into either the uncanny or the marvelous.

Eray quite consciously uses the fantastic in the service of the marvelous in order to create an alternative reality in her works. In a 2005 interview, Eray asserts, "One of the goals of the modern novel is not to describe what exists, but to create something that does not exist." She adds:

> To create a world that does not exist outside of and independently of what is being narrated, to embroider the lives of the people there, in all their richness as if they are English lace, to pull in the reader into this world, making him/her feel as if this world really exists, and then to pull the plug and put an end to it. This is writing.[7]

I would argue that this is, in fact, the way the fantastic is employed in Turkish literature of the 1980s, especially by women, who have used this mode to express their own new realities and insights in a freer, non-linear, multivalent idiom. Both Republican and post-Republican literature[8] in Turkey has focused on creating a realist tradition with believable characters that manifest psychological depth and social legibility. The project of literary realism has been linked with and has contributed immensely to the project of nation-building. Both in this political and social project and in its blueprint in the realist novel, women have held a privileged symbolic role of representing "modernity." More women began writing in Turkey after the 1950s, and by the 1980s women writers outnumbered men. These writers examined and began to write against the roles and narratives that straitjacketed them. Articulating alternative viewpoints that question socially sanctioned definitions of "reality" involved deconstructing the conventional genres and formal narrative features that encoded these social definitions. The fantastic thus emerged in the 1980s as an antidote to realism, a medium for freedom. It allows the expression of alternate realities and casts off realist constraints such as the unity of time, place, and character; the importance of motivation and psychology in characterization; and, especially in the Turkish case, the valorization of the social over the individual, of the serious over the light-hearted. Eray has been the first and most consistent practitioner of the fantastic as a genre for presenting alternate realities in contemporary Turkish literature.

While typical of Eray's style and thematic concerns, *Orpheus* occupies a special place in her oeuvre because it remains in the realm of the fantastic even at its conclusion, with no resolution towards either the uncanny or the marvelous. The narrative never adequately resolves the questions it raises or fixes the interpretations it opens up. There is a deliberate confounding of time, space, character, and motive throughout the story, and multiple coexisting interpretations are possible for each component of the narrative. Even regarding the novel's physical setting, for example—usually one of the most tangible elements of a story—in *Orpheus* there is much ambiguity and obfuscation. The story takes place in a small coastal town that undergoes rapid, sudden urbanization, but there are also indications that this may be Hell, as suggested by repeated descriptions of the overpowering and growing heat and by hints that the path to Orpheus' house might lead to the underworld. The animal Eurydice hears every night behind the bushes could be Cerberus guarding the entrance to hell. The entrance to the underworld is marked by an X on the etched stone that Mr. Night and Eurydice find in the archaeological site, associating the underworld with Orpheus' house, marked by an X on the sketch of the town. These suggestive details are never resolved, but raise questions left unanswered in the text.

There is similar ambiguity surrounding Orpheus' house and the path that approaches it. The narrator tells us repeatedly that it looks like a "space house," with its flat roof, mysteriously flashing colored lights, and the intense light that projects from it towards the end of the novel. Yet the house is also likened to an ordinary ship and is associated with the yacht that appears in the bay while Eurydice is sunbathing. This association is reinforced at several points: there is a breeze that smells of the sea around Orpheus' house; walking towards the house is likened to wading through the sea; and watching the house from the hill feels like being in a decompression chamber for divers. Eurydice's habitual night costume, her jumpsuit, is reminiscent of the typical garb of both astronauts and divers. Because of these conflicting associations, we cannot decide if Orpheus' house is under water or up in the sky—or even in a desert, as there is a sand storm towards the end. The path to Orpheus' house, likewise, can be interpreted in different ways, as conveyed by the insistence that there are several possible routes. At one level, the walk is physical and external, but it may also be internal, advancing the characters through the body of Orpheus. At first, we are told that the walk is towards the tortured soul of a troubled man, and the possibility that this journey may also be psychological is reinforced by the image of the city bus, appropriately named the "EGO."

The indeterminacy of the terrain is underlined by feelings of dread, surprise, anxiety, and fear that dominate the book. The nonresolution of these emotions keeps the reader off balance in the expectation of something big to come. The ending, however, is neither clear nor spectacular enough to provide catharsis for the accumulated tension. We never learn who Death is or why the characters did not find out more about the necropolis. The questions the book leads us to ask—why Eurydice does not simply talk to Orpheus when she finds him, or why she is unsurprised to receive a letter from a statue, for example—are forgotten by the end, as these strange details are naturalized through their repetition and easy acceptance by other characters.

However, just as the book draws to a close, these very details we have accepted are reinterpreted as strange, with Mr. Night's warning to Eurydice that Hadrian is just a statue and that she cannot know that Hadrian is in fact writing or receiving any letters. The story awakens the reader from the very lull of acceptance that it engenders. Eray thus constructs a kind of a detective novel in reverse. Whereas the process of answering questions and explaining causes leads to resolution and closure, *Orpheus* creates questions that it at first ignores, then vehemently remembers but still refuses to answer. Eray thus keeps alive the potential for multiple interpretations that is at the core of the fantastic, even as her narrative ends. In so doing, she challenges Todorov's definition of the fantastic as only a transitional genre that has to end in a certainty of one kind or another.

Intertextuality and Major Narrative Threads

Orpheus derives its primary narrative threads from intertextual references to other texts and genres. The primary narrative threads that comprise the novel are the myth of Orpheus, Bernardo Bertolucci's film *Last Tango in Paris*, the statue and life of Emperor Hadrian, the arrival of Ankara and urbanization, and the recent political history of Turkey. The interplay among these imported narrative threads allows them to animate each other and illuminate their hidden meanings. Eray allows the disparate narrative strands to stand on their own, without integrating them into a readily available or coherent whole. This lack of overt connection among the strands opens the story to different levels of interpretation while also creating a strong sense of fragmentation and sustaining Eray's use of the fantastic. In order to explore the interpretive possibilities enabled by these threads, I will consider each separately.

The Myth of Orpheus

The novel's central, unifying narrative thread is the myth of Orpheus, which has its origins in ancient Greece but has been retold in many cultures and genres, including opera, poetry, and film. The basic myth tells of Orpheus, a musician-poet who can charm animals and trees with his verse, and who can speak to the spirits. Orpheus' wife Eurydice is bitten by a snake, dies, and goes to Hades. Orpheus follows her to the underworld and persuades Hades and Persephone to let her return, on the condition that Orpheus never turn back to look at Eurydice on their journey out of Hades. As they are about to leave, Orpheus looks back at Eurydice, and she vanishes back into the underworld forever. Orpheus mourns Eurydice for a long time and, according to one version of the myth, in order to avoid a similar kind of loss, he shuns women in favor of the love of boys. This so enrages the Bacchae, female followers of Dionysus, who see it as a misogynist insult, that they tear him to pieces in a frenzy. His head and lyre float on the river Hebrus to the island of Lesbos. His severed head is buried in a shrine and becomes an oracle.

Eray's version updates and overturns the myth. The novel begins with the arrival of a sickly and anxious Eurydice, who is in search of Orpheus but upon locating him does not contact him, claiming to feel both pulled towards him and pushed away. There is something suggestively sinister about this Eurydice, with her blood from a cut finger psychologically seeping into the air, whose "blood-like" warmth seems to suffocate her. This Eurydice aims to relive the myth with the help of a mysterious figure called Mr. Night, a guide with strong eyes and nerves who might symbolically be Hades. Eurydice repeats twice that she is a woman with no past or future, and she clearly wants to move on by lifting the curse of Orpheus' backward look. Observing the gods' injunction, she carefully avoids Orpheus' gaze, watching him every night from behind his house. Yet Orpheus, now a figure with white hair and a red Alpha Romeo, feels her presence, going crazy with suffering or fear as the pulsation of lights from his house indicates.

Eurydice finally causes Orpheus' death through the intermediary of the characters in the film *Last Tango in Paris*, although she tries unsuccessfully to prevent this by stopping the film. As Jeanne kills Paul, another man whose wife has died, in the last scene of the film, Orpheus comes out of his house, which is being used as a projection screen, to be killed by Jeanne at the same time. The narrative levels of the story and the film are evened out here, so that the characters of these different texts meet and interact. Animated by Jeanne's self-defensive boldness, Eurydice, who suffers from bad eyesight, finally picks out Orpheus and looks at him as he looks at her. This reliving of the myth's climactic moment overturns its original outcome.

Last Tango in Paris

Eray uses Bertolucci's groundbreaking 1972 film as a means of opening up the original Orpheus myth, but also makes us realize that the film's plot is a kind of reverse Orpheus story. Jeanne, a twenty-year-old girl who is to marry in a week, and Paul, whose wife died the night before, have a three-day affair in an empty apartment both want to rent. Paul uses aggressive sex to purge his anger and frustration over his wife's death. Jeanne seems to go along with it because she is bored with the conventional life ahead of her; her fiancé, Tom, is filming her life for a television movie, constantly writing her into a script of conventionality and respectability. Paul at first allows Jeanne an escape from all that is scripted as he insists on not sharing anything personal, including names. But as he later realizes, standing over his dead wife's coffin, that nobody can ever know another person, he is released from the pretense of not wanting to know Jeanne and seeks a conventional, permanent relationship with her, ironically losing his appeal for her in the process. She kills him with the pistol of her colonialist father in a gesture which can be simultaneously read as conservative, nihilist, individualist, and feminist.

Eray uses the film to intimate a corporeality and sexuality missing from the novel, while connecting it to the cultural turmoil and preoccupations of the 1970s. She echoes some details of the film that connect it to the myth, such as a game Paul plays turning the lights on and off in the hotel, which resonates with Orpheus' association with light, symbolic of his ability to bring the dead from the realm of darkness to life. Turning lights on and off is also an important marker of Orpheus' presence and emotional state in Eray's story. Just as Paul and Orpheus are paired through their bereavement as widowers as well as through their association with light, Jeanne and Eurydice are also connected as doubles. Jeanne is described as a blond woman at the beginning of the script even though Maria Schneider, who plays her, is not blond. This is one of several inconsistencies between the actual movie and the published script, caused in part by the fact that the actors for whom the script was written ended up not being available to play the roles, and in part by the actors' extensive improvisation during the filming. Eray uses the gap between the film and the script to create her own version of *Last Tango in Paris*, a version in which her heroine, Eurydice, is able to be inserted into the movie, allowing the film to become the "resolution of all questions" as Eurydice promises Hadrian.

In her rewriting of the film and its script, Eray creatively accentuates Bertolucci's original text. When Eurydice reads the film script, for example, what she reads does not come directly from the actual script, but rather has been written by Eray from her experience of watching the film. She changes words and embellishes the original script with additional details that reflect what she sees on the screen.[9] Likewise, the introduction to the written version of *Last Tango in Paris* that Eurydice reads is actually assembled from two reviews of the film. The first part, referring to the acceleration of time caused by nuclear energy, comes from Norman Mailer's negative review, which was written six months after the film opened in the New York Film Festival, as a response to a positive review by Pauline Kael.[10] The pronouncements Eurydice reads that the film is revolutionary in its depiction of a primal sexuality and in the actors' use of improvisation come from Kael's original review. Thus, the text Eurydice reads combines two separate reviews that put forth diametrically opposed evaluations of the same film. Only the second and last paragraphs of the preface come from Kael's review, and the rest are from Mailer's; Eray excerpts from various portions of both reviews, disregarding context and order of argument. In borrowing from both indiscriminately, she creates an amalgam that neutralizes Mailer's criticism and subordinates his objections to Kael's judgment, which Eray obviously shares.

Eray uses the film to demonstrate her technique of borrowing, creating a collage that moves scenes out of their original order and context. Eurydice reads the script by flipping through the book randomly. At one point, the book falls and all the pages scatter on top of one another, losing their original organization. Later, when Eurydice and Mr. Night project the film onto Orpheus' house, because the handle of the projector is broken, the movie jumps from scene to scene randomly (at least from the perspective of the characters watching). Eray's technique of collage, as demonstrated by her indiscriminate juxtaposition of various pieces of the script and the film, can be described in the terms of Eurydice's experience of Ankara: as "an explosion of photographs stuck together" or "an explosion of memory." Eray's random borrowing from *Last Tango in Paris* reanimates the potentialities of the Orpheus myth: by using the collage technique to distort the original logic of the film, she defamiliarizes both the film and the context in which it is presented, allowing an alternative version of the Orpheus myth to emerge.

Emperor Hadrian

The narrative justification for the screening of *Last Tango in Paris* comes from a third central strand of *Orpheus*, the statue of Hadrian for whom Eurydice screens the film. This Roman emperor, we are told, ruled between 117 and 138 A.D. and tried to create a peaceful Roman Empire that worked more through cooperation than war. He was devoted to displaying the grandeur of his empire by building public works and architectural wonders, including his wall in northern England, his villa in Tivoli, and the Pantheon in Rome. Eray intimates this grandeur with an oblique comparison with Alexander the Great through an allusion to the knot of Gordian. In Eray's novel, Hadrian's statue, half-buried in an archaeological site behind Orpheus' house, corresponds with Eurydice through letters delivered by a carrier pigeon and emerges as a foil to Orpheus through his constancy and attentiveness to Eurydice. As she remarks, by watching Orpheus' house without interruption, the statue already does precisely what she wants to do. Corresponding with the statue serves as an outlet for Eurydice to express her worries and wishes, making her conscious of her inner thoughts. Enlivened by her emotions, the statue may in fact be the ego of Eurydice, and she admits in her final letter that in writing to him, she is writing to herself.

However, the statue is also similar to Orpheus and Paul in that the greatest tragedy of Hadrian's life was the death of his beloved Antinous. After Antinous drowned in the Nile (whether by accident, murder, or suicide), Hadrian proclaimed this young Greek boy a deity, gave his name to a star, and devoted the remaining eight years of his life to Antinous' memory. Nothing more than a head that claims expansive authority, the statue is in a way Orpheus' future. Hadrian tells Eurydice that she will either break or reinforce the bond he has with Orpheus. By causing Orpheus' death—moving him to the next stage of the myth and turning him into a severed, but talking head—Eurydice reinforces the similarity between them. The description of Orpheus' decapitated head, in Virgil's rendering at least, suggestively resembles a marble statue: "Then, too, his head was torn from his marble-white neck."[11] This image suggests a possible interpretation of Orpheus as the statue's past, and the statue as Orpheus' future.

Eray uses the statue to problematize the issue of time and the limits of historical vision. We see that even though Hadrian assures Eurydice that he knows everything about the archaeological site, he only knows of events and historical developments up until his own time. Strikingly, he needs to be told of the formation of countries like the United States or the Soviet Union, and he evaluates the present from his own imperial reality of having slaves, for example. As Marguerite Yourcenar argues in her essay "That Mighty Sculptor Time," we can never know a statue in the way it was understood in its own time.[12] Through the statue, the novel suggests that each historical period is limited by its own sensibilities and realities, even as Eray's practice of juxtaposing voices from different time periods does away with the assumption of the unity of time. Just as various kinds of space fold into each other as possible descriptions of the same location, various slices of time coexist and easily turn into each other as the novel moves among the second century of Hadrian's statue, the 1970s of the film, and 1980, as represented by the announcements Eurydice hears on the radio referring to the 1980 coup in Turkey. This fabricated temporal simultaneity is further represented in the news broadcasts from Eurydice's radio, in which news items are read together as if they occurred on the same day, when in fact they belong to different time periods—the Sicilian earthquake of 1908, for example, appears to happen on the same day as the successful creation of artificial blood, which still had not happened by 1983 when *Orpheus* was first published.

Contemporary Turkey: The Coup and Urbanization

Although the Talza coup announced on the radio is a fiction—there is no such place—a coup did take place in Turkey, on September 12, 1980, after the political polarization of the left and right escalated during the late 1970s. The period's economic crisis together with the assassinations of prominent political figures led to a widespread expectation that the army would take over. The coup occurred after skirmishes between leftist and rightist factions caused the deaths of more than 600 people in July and August of 1980, and the resulting military government was in power from 1980 until the elections of 1983. In the novel, this coup is foreshadowed when Mr. Night mentions that the date is August 12th, exactly one month before the actual coup. Eurydice later hears announcements of the military takeover and curfew on the radio. The radio announcements of the fictitious Talza coup (Talza and Turkey are connected by their initial T's) and the news that a curfew was pronounced in Rome during the shooting of Fellini's film both function as parodies of the actual coup whose effects Eurydice sees in Ankara, where a military jeep appears at the bus depot as police and soldiers line up on each side of the street. She also feels the anxiety and entrapment caused by the coup when she is lost in a maze-like Ankara. However, perceiving the world with a limited vision and awareness shaped by specific historicity, characters can only experience what their own historical period offers them. Consequently, Eurydice, who as a mythic figure belongs to the novel's most general time frame, is the only one who can witness the coup and hear the announcements of martial law.

In addition to the coup, Eray brings into her novel another phenomenon from her contemporary Turkey: urbanization. The overdevelopment of coastal towns and the resulting destruction of their natural beauty is still a topic hotly debated every summer in Turkey. Eray literalizes urbanization through the arrival of the personified city Ankara in the coastal town, a presence visually marked with the building of apartment blocks, the creation of avenues like Tunali Hilmi, and the introduction of bus service. This kind of literalization is at the core of myth-making and is the reverse side of the metaphorical function of Hadrian's statue, where his literal features are turned into abstract ideas. For example, when he complains that his hands are broken and that he is fixed in one place and consequently can only look at one thing, Eurydice consoles him by turning his predicament into a metaphor for the immobility and limited vision everybody experiences. Ankara and Hadrian demonstrate the opposite processes of literalization and abstraction, both of which are myth-making operations of language and both of which test the limits of our willingness to believe. Hadrian tells Eurydice that he is located at the boundary between belief and disbelief. By straining the limits of our suspension of disbelief, Hadrian and Ankara become the test cases of fictiveness, exposing the fictionality of all other myth figures.

Eray as Existentialist Myth-Maker

Together, the Orpheus myth, *Last Tango in Paris*, the figure of Hadrian, and the narratives of Turkey's military coup and urbanization form a narrative collage similar to the visual and aural collages represented throughout *Orpheus*. The parallels and contrasts among these strands, the connections we make between the details, allow us to read the novel in its widest matrix of myth-making. We are given the material and the means of myth-making in this book, where individual figures and their specific stories fold into each other as particular figurations of general types. Ultimately the hope for and possibility of cohesion are located in the reader, who must take up the challenge of struggling and persevering against human alienation and isolation as embodied by the fragmented text.

Eray issues this challenge indirectly through Albert Camus and his existentialist philosophy. In one of her letters to Hadrian, Eurydice mentions "A.C." as a philosopher of her age who informs her own decision to face life. Her summary of this philosophy describes Camus' idea of the absurd, best articulated in his essay "The Myth of Sisyphus." Camus argues that the acceptance of death—or of life without hope, God, or consolation—allows one to move on to real hope and a positive embracing of life. The continual awareness of death is the absurd man's burden and gift, since this awareness, which cannot be allowed to be dulled by habit, is the basis of his consciousness. Consciousness for Camus is a constant defamiliarization, or an awareness of the absurd cultivated through an unceasing cognizance and acceptance of death. He writes, "Living is keeping the absurd alive. Keeping it alive is, above all, contemplating it. Unlike Eurydice, the absurd dies only when we turn away from it."[13]

This allusion to Eurydice as the site of the absurd, which needs to be constantly gazed at, enriches our reading of Eray's Eurydice as central heroine and narrator. Eurydice is the instrument of the reader's and her own consciousness. She practices Camus' philosophy and literalizes the metaphorical meaning imbued in her figure by turning herself upon Orpheus, by claiming the position of the gazer who already knows who she is. Through the active effort of literally and figuratively pulling herself up the hill every night, she releases her life and story from the frozen and disembodied time — with no yesterday or tomorrow — in which it is locked.

Eray quotes Camus once more through the voice on the radio just before the screening of *Last Tango in Paris*. The pronouncement accompanies the torrential rain that partially washes away the heat and the atmospheric (and psychological) pressure built up in the narrative. When they turn on the radio in the jeep, the first three paragraphs Eurydice and Mr. Night hear are compiled from the opening section of Camus' essay, "Helen's Exile."[14] In Eray's rendering, this essay begins with the observation that the tragedy of the Mediterranean comes from the sun, unlike the northern tragedies, which are related to the mists. Although a slight distortion of Camus' actual words,[15] the emphasis on the sun and the Mediterranean, here and throughout the book, connects *Orpheus* to Camus' novel *The Stranger*. These associations solidify Eray's identification with Camus and her endorsement of his positions, strengthening the authority given to Camus' ideas as remedies for the dissolution and despair depicted by the film.

Camus' solution for the individual and cultural disorientation and fragmentation created by war is to recapture the idea of limits and temperance that always exists in nature and that was so celebrated by the Greeks. He writes, "Admission of ignorance, rejection of fanaticism, the limits of the world and of man, the beloved face, and finally beauty — this is where we shall be on the side of the Greeks." He insists that with the revalorization of the idea of limits, "once more the dreadful walls of the modern city will fall to deliver up — 'soul serene as the ocean's calm' — the beauty of Helen."[16] Camus uses "the beauty of Helen" here as a metonymy for an ordered, temperate, and rational life as it was epitomized by the Greeks. This is the very model he recommends as a cure for the malaise of the post-war Europeans.

However, Camus' goal of attaining "the beauty of Helen" carries with it, by implication, the requirement that one look at Helen as only a visual object, and thus conceptualizes her as a passive, abstract image rather than an active subject. Emmet Robbins writes, "One of the most prominent of recurring themes in Greek myth is the story of the recovery of an abducted princess: examples are Persephone, Helen, Eurydice." He explains that this "myth of a Maiden snatched from the embrace of Death"[17] is a remnant of an older religion that celebrated the Mother Goddess and her ability to restore the life she has taken through the dual tomb-womb function of the earth she inhabited. It takes a woman writer to restore the agency of these "abducted maidens." Instead of the Helen that Camus awaits, Eurydice—her sister—returns in Eray's story, not only to animate and restore a lost balance, but to create a specifically female order by both looking back and looking at—the past, her husband, her readers, and literature.

NOTES

[1] Now Robert College, a prestigious private high school.

[2] There is a translation at the Bogazici University site: http://www.turkish-lit. bound.edu.tr.

[3] See "Monte Kristo," in *Contemporary Turkish Literature*, ed. Talat Sait Halman (Fairleigh Dickinson University Press, 1982), 88-92; "The Underdevelopment Pharmacy," in *Short Stories by Turkish Women Writers*, trans. Nilufer Mizanoglu Reddy (Indiana University-Turkish Studies, 1994), 118-123; and "The Cellular Engineer," trans. Ozlem Sensoy, in "Cells," ed. Olivia E. Sears, special issue *TWO LINES: A Journal of Literary Translation* 8 (2001): 180-194.

[4] In its personifications of the city, the night, and a statue, *Orpheus* is reminiscent of one of Eray's earlier stories, *Geceyi Tanidim* (I Met the Night, 1979). Mr. Night in the earlier story is an African-American elevator operator from Chicago who walks with a female narrator through an anthropomorphized Chicago and out to

surrounding fields, where the narrator shows Mr. Night a statue she claims is her constant and faithful lover.

5 I have argued this in "The Discourses of the Intellectual: The Universal, the Particular and Their Mediation in the Works of Nazli Eray," *New Perspectives on Turkey* 11 (Fall 1994): 1-17.

6 Tzvetan Todorov, *The Fantastic: A Structural Approach to a Literary Genre* (Ithaca and New York: Cornell University Press, 1975), 41-57.

7 From Nazan Ozcan's interview with Eray in *Kitap* (March 8, 2005), http://www. milliyet.com.tr. The translations are mine.

8 I use these terms as chronological designators. In the Republican literature (loosely 1920-1950), the dominant preoccupation is nation-building; in the post-Republican literature (from the start of the multi-party politics until 1980), the main problematic is social justice.

9 For example, "The sound man of Tom's small crew, in fact, is recording the sonoral atmosphere" (75), becomes in Eray's text a description of the sound man, who wears earphones and kneels on the ground as he moves the microphone from left to right in order to capture the sounds of the animals.

10 Both essays are included in the published script: Bernardo Bertolucci and Franco Arcalli, *Last Tango in Paris* (New York: Delacorte Press, 1972). Pauline Kael, "Introduction," 9-19, and Norman Mailer, "A Transit to Narcissus," 199-224.

11 Quoted in W.S. Anderson, "The Orpheus of Virgil and Ovid: flebile nescio quid," in *Orpheus: The Metamorphoses of a Myth*, ed. John Warden (Toronto, Buffalo, and London: University of Toronto Press, 1982), 33.

12 Marguerite Yourcenar, "That Mighty Sculptor, Time," in *That Mighty Sculptor Time* (New York: Farrar, Straus, Giroux, 1992), 57-65. Yourcenar's biographical novel *Memoirs of Hadrian*, written as a letter from Hadrian to his adopted son Marcus Aurelius, might be the inspiration for Eray's conceptualization of the emperor and his letters.

13 Albert Camus, "The Myth of Sisyphus," in *The Myth of Sisyphus and Other Essays*, trans. Justin O'Brien (New York: Vintage International, 1991), 54.

14 Albert Camus, "Helen's Exile," in *The Myth of Sisyphus*, 185-193.

15 In O'Brien's translation, this sentence reads: "The Mediterranean sun has something tragic about it, quite different from the tragedy of fogs" (187).

16 "Helen's Exile," 192.

17 Emmet Robbins, "Famous Orpheus," in *Orpheus: The Metamorphoses of a Myth*, 9.

ORPHEUS

I had been on the bus going to the shore city I wanted to reach for almost twelve hours. My feet were swollen and I was completely exhausted. During the final two hours, I had been unable to breathe inside the bus; I had an inexplicable feeling of heaviness. I hadn't slept a wink during the whole trip.

Occasionally the bus would stop for a break, and then I would dash outside.

I went into a series of bathrooms, splashed water on my face, and looked into the mirrors.

In the mirrors, I saw a pale, tired face.

My health wasn't good. It was amazing that I would even think of taking a long trip like this, and on a bus with no air.

But everything had been planned from the start. I only got sick at the last minute.

All night long, as everyone slept on the bus, I thought of the purpose of this trip.

As we drew near the shore city, the air became warmer.

The sun came up, and my long hair stuck to the back of my neck.

The bus arrived in the city at dawn.

I was groggy from the long trip. Like the other passengers, I got off the bus walking like a crab. I waited in a spot where I could feel the warmth of the engine.

The driver's assistant gave me my blue bag.

The air was steamier than I had expected at this early hour.

I suddenly felt claustrophobic. To calm myself, I brought my hand to my throat, then scratched the nape of my neck.

The tension I felt inside increased slightly when I set foot in the shore city.

I placed my hand softly on my neck above my collarbone; my outfit had become grimy during the night bus trip.

I pushed back the hair stuck to my forehead and flagged down a taxi; I told the driver the name of the hotel I wanted.

The city was still sleeping.

The taxi passed along a dusty street and dropped me off in front of the hotel. The driver placed my blue bag in front of the door; after I gave him his money, he took off.

I was so tired I could hardly stand up. I told the man at the reception desk my name.

"Your room is ready, number ten," he said. "The bellboy will bring your bag up right away."

"I wonder if there are any messages for me," I asked.

He turned and looked at the pigeonhole for number ten. He found a little piece of paper.

"Yes, a Mr. Night left a note for you. He says to call," he said.

"Thanks. Where's the phone?" I asked.

He pointed over to where the phone was.

Then he went into the back of the hotel, towards the kitchen. He took out bottles of water and fruit juice from a case that had obviously just arrived and began to line them up on the white tiles.

A young boy appeared and began to carry my bag upstairs to my room.

I asked the man at the reception desk for a bottle of water. My throat was quite dry.

"Put it on my bill," I said.

"Yes, of course, ma'am," he replied.

He turned back to his work.

I opened the bottle; the water was warm. I gulped it down. When I opened the bottle, I cut my thumb a little, as I always do.

With the key to my room in my hand, I got my telephone book out of my dust-covered purse.

I found my assistant's telephone number.

Mr. Night!

What an interesting name he had chosen for himself.

I dialed the number. The telephone rang for a long time. My finger was bleeding a little. As I sucked on it, he answered the phone.

"Hello," said the voice on the other end.

"Good morning. I'm afraid I've woken you up. I just got into town and came to the hotel. I got your note. Where did you find the name 'Mr.

Orpheus

Night?' It's interesting," I said.

My assistant answered from the other end: "I thought it was the right name for me," he said, and laughed.

"Wonderful," I said. "I'm going to run up to my room in a minute and go to sleep. That long trip tired me out. All the plans are ready. When can I meet with you?"

My assistant—and this was a person whom I had never seen before, who had, in addition, chosen a very unique name—knew me and knew, more or less, the plans that I had set out.

"You get a good rest. Get rid of all that exhaustion from the long trip. I'll be at your hotel at five o'clock," he said.

"Fine," I said. "I already know that your eyes are very strong, that you can see well in the dark, and that you are extraordinarily logical. I'll be able to give you more details little by little in the next few days, as I get used to the climate of the city and relax. My eyes don't see very well. And I can't see at all at night. I can't pick out what I need to, in other words. On top of everything, I'm very emotional. I can mix everything up in a second. I'm relying on your logic. You're my assistant. Well, we can talk about this in detail when you come to the hotel at five o'clock. Take care for now."

My assistant said, "See you at five o'clock at your hotel."

I hung up the telephone.

I went up to my room on the second floor. They had left my bag in front of the door; I brought it inside.

It was covered with dust. I blew away the dust, then opened the zipper and took out my towel. I was incapable of even putting my things away in the closet.

Inside me that strange tension continued, along with a weariness difficult to describe.

I lit a cigarette.

The hot air of the city began to fill the room. I pulled the curtains back and closed them.

I sat on the bed and finished my cigarette.

I took a warm shower. Then I lay down and stretched out on the bed.

I took my wristwatch off and placed it on the night table.

I thought a little.

My feet were swollen. I stared at them for a while. Then I fell asleep.

(At this point, I should thank my assistant, who is a real person, not simply a character in a novel, who had chosen the name Mr. Night for himself.

Actually, none of the people in these events are fictitious characters. As for my assistant, who called himself Mr. Night, I never saw him again.

Yet, in that summer season in the shore city, he served as my common sense, my judgment, my ears and my eyes.

He accepted the position as my assistant.

Why, I still don't know ...

Perhaps I had unwittingly inserted him into this unusual universe with which I needed to come to terms.

He knew that somewhere on the boundaries of perception, I was playing with dreams and reality.

In these lines, I wanted to thank my assistant for his considerable help in my reliving of the Orpheus myth.)

... I took off my wristwatch and placed it on the night table.

I thought a little.

My feet were very swollen. I stared at them for a while.

I was a person whose yesterday had been taken away and who had no tomorrow.

I knew this.

But my dreams were extraordinary.

As the sun warmed my room, I fell asleep, exhausted by the trip and the warm air.

I woke up before five. I wasn't really refreshed, but I felt better than when I arrived in the city in the morning.

There was only a little time before I would see my assistant.

I got ready.

At exactly five o'clock, dressed in my jumpsuit and summer sandals with thin straps, I went to the reception.

I had given my hair a good combing, and it hung down below my shoulders.

I had also put on some good perfume, my old habit.

In the reception area, I immediately picked out my assistant, whom I had never seen or met before.

There was nobody else nearby anyway.

My assistant stood there with no expression on his face. I think he was young, but it was hard to tell his age at first glance. He was dressed in white.

He was sitting in an armchair smoking a cigarette.

He put out the cigarette and stood up.

He recognized me.

Smiling, I shook his hand.

"Good morning, Mr. Night. I hope I didn't keep you waiting. That long trip really did me in. And the air in this shore city is hotter than I expected at this season ...

"And how are you?" I asked.

My assistant asked how I felt. It was then that I understood that he was young, very young.

"When I was talking to you on the phone, I said that I would give you some information. We should find someplace where we can speak comfortably. I will tell you part of the plan little by little. If you don't mind, I'd like to ask you some questions first."

My assistant was relaxed and quick.

"Okay. The lobby's completely empty right now. I think we could sit in the back and speak comfortably," he said.

We went to the corner he had proposed.

We sat across from one another at the table.

We were following one another with our eyes.

I realized that he was waiting, so I began to speak.

"Mr. Night," I said. "I'm going to call you that for now because I like it—how well you have figured out one part of what's going on.

"I think we'll only work at night.

"Let's get to my questions. Actually, I'm quite concerned about certain things. May I ask you about them?" I said.

He smiled.

"Please ask," he said.

"Mr. Night, why do you want to get involved in this very questionable matter, even though you don't know who I am?" I asked.

He smiled again.

"I know you a little. I'm not afraid of danger. That's why I wanted to be your assistant. And if you really consider the situation, the danger's rather abstract. Like everything else ... I don't know. Was I able to answer your question?" he said.

Each of us lit a cigarette.

I thought for a moment.

"Yes, you answered my first question. I understand you. And, as things develop, you will get to know me better. But there's one thing still bothering me.

"Have you ever considered that I might be crazy? A person who would start something like this might very well be crazy. Haven't you ever thought of this?" I asked.

Mr. Night laughed again.

"No, I know you're not crazy," he said.

I laughed too.

"How can you be so sure I'm not crazy?" I asked.

"No," said Mr. Night. "You're not crazy."

I put my cigarette out.

"Good, let's leave it at that," I said.

He trusted both me and himself, I understood.

I had asked the bellboy to bring us some fruit juice. As my assistant and I sipped our juice, I continued to ask him questions.

I lit up another cigarette and asked him the most important question.

"What do you know about Orpheus?"

Mr. Night was quiet for a moment.

"I know very little. In fact, you could say that I know practically nothing about Orpheus. I don't mean the Orpheus of mythology. I mean the Orpheus that we're after. I know very little about him ..." he said.

"He's a person, like you and me," I said.

"Isn't he a dream?" asked my assistant.

"No," I said. "No, he's not a dream. Little by little I'll explain him to you," I said.

Mr. Night was intrigued. I was observing him too. I suddenly saw the winds of different emotions passing across his face.

He thought a little.

"Then Orpheus is in this shore city right now," he said.

"Yes," I replied.

Mr. Night suddenly seemed to sit up straight.

"Okay, then Eurydice? Where's Eurydice? Orpheus' dead lover ..." my assistant asked.

"We don't know yet whether she's dead or alive. Perhaps she ran here to die. Perhaps there is no Eurydice ... Look, this is a possibility ...

Orpheus

We could only be in search of Orpheus. An Orpheus with no Eurydice in his life," I said.

My assistant was taken aback.

"This is really scary ... Well, what about death? There's death in this game too, isn't there? Because there is death in the story of Orpheus and Eurydice," he said.

As this conversation took place between us, I had been carefully examining his face.

He was sensitive.

"Yes, there's death," I said.

He stopped for a moment.

"Where?" he asked.

"Oh, Mr. Night, you ask very good questions! Death is always there, everywhere, all the time," I said.

My assistant passed his hand lightly over his forehead.

"I know. But I asked about the death in this game," he said.

I kept silent.

He asked: "Well, where is that 'death'?"

"It's here too, Mr. Night. It's in this shore city too," I said.

I was looking at him again. He was clearly upset, but he was trying not to show it.

"I have to ask you one last thing," he said.

"Ask," I said.

"Who is death?" asked my assistant.

Again I kept silent for a bit. For a little while now, I had been continually examining his face.

"Mr. Night, I don't know who death is either," I said.

He ran his hands through his hair.

"Is it you?" he asked.

I laughed. I took a sip of fruit juice.

"No, it's not me. So is it you?" I asked, laughing.

Mr. Night quickly responded: "No, it's not me. I'm your assistant. I'm not death."

The tension I felt inside increased, but at the same time I felt somehow happy.

"I know you're not death, don't be upset," I said.

I leaned towards him from where I sat. I came a little closer to him.

"What we're playing is a game with death. So neither you nor I could be death, right?" I asked.

"Yes," said my assistant in a calm voice.

I ordered another bottle of fruit juice for each of us.

"Look, Mr. Night," I said. "At this moment in this shore city there's Orpheus, there's death, there's you—my assistant—and there's me. And that's all we know for now.

"Listen to me. Could you sketch a detailed plan of this shore city? As far as I can see, the things we actually know right now aren't going to get us very far. For us to find Orpheus more easily we absolutely must have a plan. I don't know the roads and goat trails at all. At this point I don't know anyplace here other than our hotel and this road.

"Our time is limited. Orpheus could descend into the Underworld at any moment to find his lover Eurydice ...

"Look, I just thought of something else. We'll have to keep watch at the post office too. I think Orpheus might try to telephone from the post office even to a Eurydice who doesn't exist. I think he'll try to telephone the other world. He'll keep trying her, Eurydice, from different telephones. Those lines with a lot of static can connect to the other world, but if Eurydice's not there, he won't be able to talk to her. He could run into some bad tempered operator. And in the end he might want to go there.

"We'll follow him there. We have to find out where he's staying by tomorrow at the latest. Okay?" I asked.

"Okay. I'll draw the plan of the city tonight. It's just a little place anyway," he said.

I thanked my assistant.

"Come to the hotel tomorrow when it gets dark," I said.

My assistant stood up.

"I'll come here tomorrow at 8:00. The sketch will be ready. Wear flat shoes," he said.

We said goodbye.

Just as we were parting, I said: "Mr. Night, I'll wear flat shoes and a comfortable outfit. Would you wear a dark color? You know, the night has a thousand eyes."

"Have no fear," he said.

I went up to my room. I opened my suitcase and placed my things in the wardrobe in the corner. I had brought a pair of espadrilles. I placed them next to my other shoes. I picked up my little binoculars and looked at them. I could have brought a useful pair of adjustable binoculars. But instead I had brought a little pair of opera glasses covered with mother-of-pearl.

If necessary my assistant could use them.

I was hungry.

I took my room key in my hand. It was a key like any other.

I played with it a little, then went down to the hotel dining room.

As I ate, I was continually thinking ...

I went to bed early that night. I had little time. I had to use it well. At one point I became afraid when I thought I might be too late.

Then I undressed and went to bed. I turned my back to the wall and slept.

I woke up early. I was very refreshed. As soon as I woke up, I lit up a cigarette and asked for some tea in my room. I drank three glasses of tea one after the other.

I felt great.

I didn't leave my room all day, but I sat on the balcony for a bit; I was trying to make myself adjust to the heat, to the climate of this shore city.

Towards eight o'clock I tied my hair up in a bun and put on my espadrilles and my dark jumpsuit.

I was looking down from my balcony; I saw my assistant Mr. Night coming straight towards the hotel.

I took my little purse with me; I glanced quickly around my room to see if I had forgotten anything. I had forgotten my pack of cigarettes on the balcony. I tossed them into my purse, locked the door, and went down to the reception.

My assistant was there.

He was waiting where he had sat the day before. I looked and saw he was in a very good mood this evening. I shook his hand.

"How are you? How did your day go?" I asked.

"It went very well. Everything's just fine," he said.

"Were you able to sketch the plan?" I asked.

"Yes, I drew it up. And I drew it with a lot of detail," he said.

"Oh, great. Let's look at it right away. I wonder where we can look at it? This really isn't the place," I said.

"Yes," said Mr. Night. "I thought about that too. It can't be here. There's a kind of run-down tea garden on the shore; let's go there. I have things I want to tell you," he said, and laughed.

I was intrigued.

We walked towards the tea garden my assistant had selected.

He really had made a good choice. There was absolutely no one around. Once in a while a dead wave slapped against the shore. We sat at a table near the sea. We ordered two teas. My assistant got out the plan and spread it on the table. The shore city was truly very small. I leaned down and looked at it closely. The plan was very detailed and beautifully drawn.

"You've drawn the city plan very expertly, Mr. Night. Or are you a city planner? You see, I don't know what you really do," I said.

"No," he said. "I'm not a city planner. And I'm not an architect. But I worked very carefully on the sketch the whole day ..."

I was thinking about what he was going to tell me.

Just then the waiter brought the tea.

I waited for him to go away, then I turned to my assistant.

"You were going tell me something. You said so in the lobby of the hotel! I'm waiting," I said.

He took a sip of his tea. I took a sip too. I was watching him carefully.

He said: "I've found Orpheus' house."

My mouth became dry.

"Yes, I know where Orpheus' house is. And I also found out that he has a red Alpha Romeo," he said.

I was really astonished that he worked so quickly.

I finished my tea in one gulp.

"How did you learn all this, Mr. Night?" I asked.

"I researched it," he said. "I researched it very well. There are people who know him in this shore city. They don't know him very well ... For example, they don't even know that he's Orpheus."

I was so excited that I couldn't stay in my chair.

I stood up and looked at the sea.

A thousand thoughts were racing through my mind in that instant.

I sat down again.

"An Alpha Romeo is a very fast car! We have to use our time very well. What else did you learn?" I asked.

My assistant ordered two more teas.

He too was looking at the sea while he spoke.

"I couldn't find out whether or not Orpheus is in his house at the moment," he said.

"Where is his house?" I asked.

The waiter brought the teas. We waited for him to disappear.

"The house is far away, up in the hills," said Mr. Night.

I was very excited.

Mr. Night was looking closely at me.

"Could you show me the location of the house on this plan?" I asked.

He pointed with his forefinger to an X at the end of a goat trail.

I looked closely at it.

My tea had become cold.

I was still looking at the plan.

"So he has a red Alpha Romeo ..." I said.

"Yes," said my assistant.

I made a quick decision.

"Tonight is a moonless night. I wonder if we'll be able to find the house in the darkness ... If we look from behind, from four hundred meters away, we'll be able to tell whether he's at home or not. What do you say?" I said.

Mr. Night looked up at the hills.

"The house is in a steep place. You have to go around a lot of curves and turns to get there. But if you think you're strong enough, we can go," he said.

"I'm very strong tonight. I'm curious about the house. Is Orpheus there, I wonder? The Alpha Romeo scares me. He could go anywhere at any moment ... You understand, don't you?" I asked.

"Yes," said my assistant. "I understand you very well. Calm down. I know you can't see well in the darkness. You told me that. We'll be looking at the house from very far away, from behind."

My assistant's words relaxed me.

My spirits picked up.

I asked the waiter for a piece of toast.

"I forgot to tell you. I'm afraid of dogs," I said.

"Don't be afraid," said Mr. Night. "The dogs around here don't bother people."

"It doesn't matter, it's not something I can control. I'm still afraid of dogs," I said.

"I know. You're afraid of just one dog. That's the dog Cerberus*
who waits at the door of the Underworld, isn't it, Miss Eurydice?" my
assistant said.

I was astonished all over again.

"How did you know that I was Eurydice?" I said.

"I've known it from the start. Nobody other than me knows this ..."
said my assistant.

"And Orpheus knows," I said.

"Yes," said Mr. Night. "He knows too."

"You're worried. You're afraid that something will happen to him,
aren't you, Miss Eurydice? Isn't that it?" my assistant asked.

I looked down in front of me.

"Yes," I said.

What else could I say?

"But on the other hand, 'death' is after you; you know that too, don't
you?" he said.

He knew everything.

I didn't quite know what to say.

"That's not so important," I said.

It had grown dark.

My assistant said: "Tonight we're going. There are things you want
to see. You'll see them with my eyes. And as I said, don't be afraid of
anything," he said.

I was so excited that I couldn't breathe.

Sitting next to me, my assistant was speaking calmly.

"Now we're going to Orpheus' house. But if you're going to be so
excited, we'll never make it there. Listen to me and calm down. Look,
we're going to be four hundred meters away from him tonight," he said.

My assistant was much more powerful than I had thought. Now I
understood that.

"Okay, from this moment on I'm leaving everything to you, Mr.
Night," I said to him.

We quietly passed into the darkness.

We were climbing up along a series of roads that Mr. Night knew
well, that he had expertly found on the map, pausing along the way.

---

*The original Turkish text uses the name "Argus" for the dog. In the Greek myth,
Cerberus is the dog who guards the Underworld; Argus, or Argos, is the name of
Odysseus' dog in *The Odyssey*.

The road in front of us was winding and long. The sky was filled with stars. Every once in a while, we would stop to sit on a wall and have a cigarette.

At one point a star shot across the huge sky.

"Mr. Night, Mr. Night, did you see that?" I shouted.

He had become much quieter since we had entered into the night.

"Yes, I saw it. There are a lot of shooting stars in the sky here. I think you can see one or two shooting stars every night," he said.

In the darkness we were going straight towards a person whose soul was riddled with contradictions, and I had left finding the roads to Mr. Night.

Mr. Night paused for a moment at a fork in the road.

"I'm going to take you to Orpheus' house by a very unique route. If you want to look at his house from behind and far away, it would be best for us to take that road," he said.

We went off onto a twisting, turning road that rose and fell. We walked on for a while longer. I was out of breath.

Finally we came out upon a flat, open area.

The sky was filled with stars. The distant sounds of insects filled my ears. The air was as hot as blood.

Mr. Night said: "Be careful. There are thorns on the ground. They could stick you in the foot. They're poisonous thorns that cause swelling and itching where they pierce."

I was walking next to my assistant, examining the ground with great care as I went.

We walked on for a long time like this. I was very tired, and just as I was about to turn and say, "Let's sit and rest for a bit," Mr. Night turned to me: "Well, there's Orpheus' house ... Four hundred meters away from us. That building you can see in the darkness ..." he said.

I thought my heart would stop.

I was trembling.

I looked at the place Mr. Night indicated.

At first I didn't see anything.

Unfortunately, my eyes weren't as strong as his.

I was slowly trying to accustom my eyes to the distant darkness.

The shadow I could perceive in the distance must have been the back of the house.

Suddenly a light went on in the house.

"Mr. Night, Orpheus is in his house," I said.

"Yes," he said. "And the Alpha Romeo is parked there behind the house."

"Please let's sit down over there. I saw the light. I can't see the car. But the light is there all right," I said.

I could no longer stand up. I collapsed to the ground.

Mr. Night was looking at the house as if his eyes were fixed to invisible binoculars.

What could he see from so far away?

I couldn't even see the Alpha Romeo.

Suddenly the light went out.

Mr. Night said softly: "I see Orpheus. He's sitting motionless in the darkness."

I couldn't see Orpheus at all.

Mr. Night looked more carefully.

"Yes, without moving," he said.

"Oh, Mr. Night, you can see him, so why can't I see him," I complained.

"Wait," said my assistant. "Let your eyes get used to the darkness and maybe you'll be able to see him."

"Isn't he moving at all?" I asked.

"Strange. Not at all," said Mr. Night.

The air was murderously hot. I wiped the sweat off my forehead with the back of my hand.

"I wonder, do you think he can sense my presence, feel that I'm so close by?" I asked.

He laughed softly.

"You'd know that best," he said.

I changed my sitting position. A thorn stuck me through my cloth shoes. I felt a sudden pain.

"We're in a dangerous place. If you ask me, they probably consider this to be outside the city limits," I said.

Mr. Night continued to stare into the darkness without moving his eyes.

"Orpheus got up," he said.

Suddenly all the lights in the house went on.

I was terrified.

"Yes, maybe he sensed you," said Mr. Night.

Orpheus

I saw a house like a space house. It was very far away, and I couldn't see it well.

Orpheus was inside the house. It was very likely that he was walking from room to room.

I was afraid.

At that moment, I became afraid.

"Let's go, Mr. Night. Please, let's get out of here," I said.

"Okay," said Mr. Night. "Orpheus is wandering around in the house ... Let's go."

I was covered with sweat. I stood up. We ran back to the hotel.

Before he left, I said to my assistant: "Sleep well, Mr. Night. See you tomorrow night."

There was no one in the lobby. It must have been very late. I leaned over and took my key. I went up to my room. I washed my face. I got undressed and lay down on my bed.

I hadn't seen Orpheus, but I'd seen his house that looked like a space house, I'd seen his loneliness, his lights.

Orpheus ... I had found him.

I woke up in the morning to a rapping on my door.

I waited for a moment, eyes open, in my bed.

There was another knock on the door to my room. This time it was more powerful. I looked at my watch on the night table. It was only eight o'clock. I got up from my bed and slowly opened the door a little.

The bellboy from the reception desk had come: "Ankara's calling you, ma'am," he said.

A call from Ankara! Who was it, I wondered?

"Fine, I'm coming right down," I said to the boy.

I looked hastily around for something to put on, threw on my jumpsuit, and dashed to the phone.

"Hello," I said.

"Hello," said the voice at the other end.

"With whom am I speaking, please?" I asked.

The voice on the other end of the phone said: "Don't you recognize me? I'm Ankara. The place you're from. The place you live, Ankara."

That old hag of a city I'd spent fifteen years with, back to belly, Ankara herself, was on the phone with me.

This was impossible!

But I know Ankara very well. You can expect anything from her!

"Ankara, what do you want?" I asked in a polite tone.

And of course she replied: "I'm coming to the shore city too. I'll be there with you. I just thought I'd let you know."

"Please Ankara," I said slowly. "Are you crazy? And how would you get here? It's just a little shore city. Stay where you are."

The city on the other end of the phone laughed with that raspy voice.

"I'm coming on the noon plane. On the plane called Ankara," she said.

I had no idea what to do. Ankara was coming to the shore city on the "Ankara," that's all.

Suddenly I thought of something: "Ankara, you won't fit here. And you can't fit on the plane. Do you want to ruin everything?" I asked.

The city came out with another laugh: "I'll fit on the plane, and I'll fit there too. Don't get all upset. Do you want anything? One of my universities, the railroad station, a park, and a traffic circle with flowers, any of my streets, the MESA apartments? Do you need a bus or anything there? For God's sake, don't be shy. Tell me. I'll bring it with me."

Standing there at the telephone, I had no idea what to say.

I asked the city a crazy question.

"Fine, did you get your airplane ticket?" I said.

Ankara gave out another shriek of laughter from the other end of the phone.

"Of course I have it. I made a reservation yesterday and picked it up today. What do you want from here? Tell me that," she said.

Things were getting serious.

"Ankara," I said. "Why do you want to come here? Do you think I ran away from you? Look, I have important things to do here … If you come here, everything's going to get all mixed up … In any event, what you're proposing is simply impossible. I've never heard of one city coming to another. This is madness," I said.

Ankara said: "There are a lot of new developments being set up along the shore. Half of Ankara's there anyhow. You have no idea. I'll come and quietly settle down there. Of course I'm not going to come inside that little shore city; but I'm coming close by. I've got a place ready with all the paperwork done.

"I don't understand why you're so upset. Since it's by the sea, no one will figure out that I'm Ankara. Haven't you seen all that awful urban development going up like mushrooms all around you? And I was just thinking I'd be near you. I'll change my color. Don't worry. And I'll make a bet with you, my dear friend that no one will even notice that I'm Ankara."

I saw there was no way out.

The city was coming.

On the noon plane!

"Ankara, at least don't bring a lot of things with you. Forget the universities and all that. Please don't bring the post office, the Parliament, I don't know, the markets, the malls, Ulus Square, the skyscrapers," I said.

She was pleased.

"Ah, see you finally understand me. I just thought I'd bring one or two of your favorite little streets."

"Please forget about the streets. Bring one or two plots of land. A small restaurant. Settle down without anybody seeing you," I said.

"All right," said the city. "Oh, I'll go in the sea and cool off. You'll be more relaxed too, with me nearby. After all, you've gotten used to me all these years," she said.

"This is still madness!" I said.

"No. If you think carefully, you'll understand that this isn't madness but reality," she said.

I was worn out.

"Okay, see you," I said.

The Ankara line was cut just then anyway.

This event had both astonished and exhausted me.

I had to tell my assistant right away. So Ankara, the great city of the plains, had taken it into her head and was coming to the shore city on the noon plane.

I said to the bellboy, who had emerged from the kitchen with a coffee tray in his hand: "May I make a phone call? Put it on my account before you forget," I said.

"Of course, ma'am," he said.

I dialed my assistant's number. He picked up on the second ring.

"How are you?" I asked. "Excuse me for calling you so early in the morning, but an unbelievable thing has happened. I thought I should tell you," I said.

My assistant said: "I was sunbathing on the terrace. I worried about you all night long. You haven't come across some life-threatening danger, have you?" he asked.

I laughed.

"Don't worry, it has nothing at all to do with death. Let me tell you what happened," I said.

My assistant was very excited.

"Listen," I said. "Ankara called me up a little while ago. No, not a friend from Ankara, but the city itself called me. Yes, it's strange, very strange, but the more I think about it, the more natural what she said begins to seem to me. Yes … the city of the plains is coming on the noon plane to the shore city. 'They won't even notice. You'll see,' she said to me. 'You don't know about urbanization,' she said. She asked if I wanted anything. It seems she's going to settle down somewhere nearby. I told her to bring very little with her. I asked her to bring a good restaurant and a nice piece of land. I hope she doesn't bring anything else," I said.

Mr. Night was very surprised at first. Then he said: "Well, what the city says is right from one point of view. Let her come and then we'll see. If she settles down quietly in some far-away corner …"

"Yes," I said. "Yes, I think so too. I wanted to let you know. I was surprised at first too, but now everything seems somehow normal …"

"Mr. Night, I'll see you in the hotel at eight tonight."

"All right," he said. "I looked at the plan again last night. I saw new things. Wear your flat shoes again."

"Yes, I'll wear my flat shoes. Now I'm going up to my room, and I want to sunbathe on my balcony."

I said goodbye to my assistant and hung up the telephone.

I went up to my room.

Getting undressed again, I stretched out on my bed. It was hard for me to sleep during the day. The air of the shore city was getting hotter and hotter. I closed all the curtains. The inside of the room became a little cooler. My room got the morning sun.

Before I went to bed, I got out my bathing suit and sun cream from my suitcase and put them next to my towel.

Towards noon, I woke up from a very light sleep. I rang the bell, called the bellboy, and asked for a double tea.

The place where the thorn had pierced me the night before was red and swollen. It was obvious the thorn was still under my skin.

As I looked at my foot, I thought of the walk the night before and Orpheus' house that I had seen from afar in the darkness.

How all those lights had suddenly turned on!

There was a tapping at the door. I opened it. The bellboy had brought the tea.

"Put the tray on the balcony," I said.

The bellboy placed the tea tray on the table on the balcony.

"Should they change the sheets every day, ma'am? And should they clean the room every day?" he asked.

The bellboy was a nice adolescent with just the beginnings of a moustache; he still seemed like a child.

"It'll be fine if they clean my room every other day and change the sheets every day. Is it going to get hotter? Do you know?" I asked him.

"Yes, they're expecting both the sea and the air temperature to rise," he said.

"Ma'am, you know what, they started to build a new development site near us. I heard about it at noon. It's going to be a very different kind of place," he said.

"It's very interesting. They keep on starting new development sites in the area. I'm afraid they're going to ruin this lovely shore city," I said.

"I don't know, ma'am, but for us who come from around here it's really something, all these new places around here," the boy said.

He said goodbye and left the room.

Just as I sat on the wicker chair on the balcony and took a sip of tea, there was a tapping at the door.

I got up and opened it.

I saw it was the bellboy again. He had obviously run up the stairs, as he was out of breath.

"Ankara's calling you," he said.

I left my tea on the balcony, went downstairs, and took the receiver in my hand.

It was Ankara again, with that smoky, raspy voice.

"Hello," she said from the other end.

"Hello," I said.

"I'm here," she said.

"I know, I guessed so. The bellboy at the hotel told me," I said.

The city came out with a deep laugh again.

"So, I'm here. I'm settling in. And it's so beautiful here. I love it. The plane bounced around a little on the way here, but no harm done. I

brought you a plot of land or two, a good restaurant, a notary public—
oh, and Tunali Hilmi Avenue," she said.

She was full of fun.

Quietly, I said: "What! You brought Tunali Hilmi Avenue, the whole
street and all those people?"

"No, no, just a part of it. When I get settled in here, you're going to
love Tunali Hilmi Avenue. I'm just getting settled in now. I'll get in touch
with you from the hotel. I'm thinking of putting Tunali Hilmi Avenue
right on the water's edge. What do you think?" she asked.

What should I say?

"Not bad," I said.

I hung up the phone.

I went up to my room again.

Ankara had brought Tunali Hilmi Avenue as well. How long would
it take her to settle in, I wondered?

I put on my bathing suit and went out on the balcony. It was just
the right time for sunbathing. I spread sun cream on my arms and legs,
spread my towel on the ground, and stretched out.

Since I had arrived from the city, my body had not seen the sun;
it was completely white. From where I lay, I occasionally turned and
looked at the sea.

It was really getting hot. I went inside for a minute and pressed the
bell next to the bed. The bellboy came running.

"Bring me a Pepsi with lemon and ice," I said.

"Of course, ma'am," said the bellboy. "I'll bring it right away."

I went out on the balcony again and looked at the sea.

Suddenly a red Alfa Romeo passed in front of the hotel. I jumped up
in excitement, bent far over the iron railing, and stared after it.

Strangely, for a few seconds, I saw a man dressed in white with
white hair at the wheel.

Was it possible that there were two red Alpha Romeos of the same
model in the shore city? Or did someone else use Orpheus' car once in a
while?

I was disoriented and confused.

There was a tapping at the door.

"Come in," I said.

The bellboy came in carrying a tray with the Pepsi on it.

"Put those things in the shade," I said.

The bellboy left the tray on the little table. Just as he went out the door, he said: "Ma'am, do you know, that development site I told you about earlier is growing incredibly fast. They're laying out a big avenue right on the seaside. I'm getting really excited."

"Interesting, interesting, where are you getting this news?" I asked him.

The bellboy said: "My friends saw it when they were fishing, ma'am. They're setting up the light poles on the avenue and everything," he said.

After the bellboy left, I thought for a moment. It seemed that Ankara had already begun to set up Tunali Hilmi!

I sipped my Pepsi-Cola under the sun. This first time I had been out during the day had tired me. I slept until 7:30.

I got up and dressed. My mind was fixated on the red Alpha Romeo that had passed in front of the hotel, and how quickly Ankara had settled into the shore city.

There were a lot of things I had to tell Mr. Night about.

I put on my flat cloth shoes and my jumpsuit. I left the Pepsi glass and the tray outside my door. I picked up my small bag and my cigarettes and matches, ran a comb through my hair, and went down to the reception.

I was late; Mr. Night had come and was sitting in his usual place.

I hurried over to him: "Good evening, Mr. Night. As I told you on the phone, things have happened and I'm just dazed. Excuse me, I've kept you waiting," I said.

Mr. Night said politely, as usual: "No, of course not, you didn't keep me waiting, I've just come myself. The bellboy was telling me with much excitement about the new development sites springing up everywhere. I listened to him a little. Of course I knew very well about 'whom' he was talking," he said.

"Mr. Night," I said. "Do you know what I saw from my balcony today? A red Alpha Romeo passed in front of the hotel very quickly. But I couldn't really pick out who was driving. It seemed like someone with graying hair. He turned off and went straight uphill. Could there be two Alpha Romeos?" I asked.

Mr. Night was equally surprised.

"Very interesting," he said. "There's just one Alpha Romeo ..."

He was thinking ...

"It's really very strange. The only Alpha Romeo I know of is Orpheus'. With five gears."

I was dumbfounded.

"Did you say five gears, Mr. Night?" I shouted.

Mr. Night said: "Yes, five gears, and it goes very fast."

I was upset. Mr. Night was very calm.

"Anyway, look, I can think of other things we should be concentrating on. Maybe we should do a time comparison. We didn't think of that until now. For example, at what time did you see the red car?" he asked.

I thought. I didn't know exactly.

"I think it was about 5:30 or so ... But I'm not sure," I said to my assistant.

He was thinking again.

"Maybe Orpheus isn't alone right now. He could have had a friend with him. But I think he was alone when we saw him last night. Because he was sitting there completely still. It didn't seem like there was a guest in the house. You couldn't see, but I saw very well. Yes, I'm sure he was alone. You're excited. Are you sure you didn't make a mistake? Didn't you perhaps see Orpheus?" my assistant asked.

"I'm sure. It wasn't Orpheus at the wheel, Mr. Night," I said.

My assistant stood up.

"Well, in any event, I think we'll learn the truth about a number of things better tonight. Orpheus' house is the kind of building where you can hardly see anything when you look from behind. But you want to look from behind ... We weren't able to stay there very long last night because you got upset ..." he said.

"Mr. Night, we're going to see him from four hundred meters away and from behind again. See, I'm very calm now," I said.

"Come on. Let's go. We have a long way to go, you know," said my assistant.

"All right, Mr. Night, let's go," I said.

With Mr. Night at my side, I set off into the dark, hot streets.

We were walking pretty quickly again, stopping occasionally to sit on a wall and have a cigarette.

Ours was a strange journey. It gripped my attention. It was as though we were trying to get to a man by making our way through the labyrinth inside him.

"As I told you before, tonight we're going by a different road to get there," said Mr. Night.

"Would you believe, I paid no attention. This shows how absent-minded I am."

"But there's also the factor of my not being able to see in the dark. Besides, all the roads seem exactly the same. Believe me, that wall that we just sat on to have a cigarette seemed like the same wall that we sat on last night," I said.

My assistant laughed: "Yes, it is the same wall. We still haven't turned onto the new road," he said.

"You find a new road every day. How strange, I thought there was only one road to Orpheus' house," I said.

He laughed.

"How could there ever be only one road? I think we'll find any number of other roads that lead there," he said.

Again I heard the sounds of insects.

Again the night was as warm as blood.

Suddenly I realized that the road had changed.

Mr. Night said: "Walk carefully. We're coming to the house through an archaeological site this time. There are thistles here, but mostly just stones. You might trip on a rock. The archaeological site we're passing through right now belongs to a very old civilization. They excavated and conducted research here until quite recently.

"Right now we're passing across the excavation site. I know you'll get excited, but they found one or two Roman graves in the excavation. They were empty," he said.

My assistant was quite right. I was excited.

"But Mr. Night," I said. "Graves don't frighten me. But did you know that I'm very interested in archaeology? For example, statues ... Statues intrigue me. Were there any statues found in this excavation, I wonder? Well, anyway, if they did find any they would have taken them off to the museum. Isn't that right?" I asked.

We continued to walk on.

The whole area was full of stones left from centuries ago.

It was really quite difficult to walk in the darkness in this archaeological site.

Mr. Night was looking straight ahead. He answered my question in a low voice: "How strange. You already knew what I was going to say to you. Yes, they dug up a number of statues in this excavation. As you said, most are now in the museum. They only left one of them in place, because they were afraid it would shatter. We're going to look at the house from next to the statue now. It's always looking at Orpheus' house ..."

I was so surprised that I tripped over a rock and almost fell.

"Please, Mr. Night, what are you telling me? Whose statue is this that continually stares at the back of Orpheus' house, from four hundred meters away?" I asked.

Mr. Night said: "Don't get impatient. You'll see when we get there. Anyway, we're very near," he said, and added nothing else.

We walked a little more among the stones in the windless, blood-hot night.

Suddenly I saw the statue.

It took me so much by surprise, I almost bumped into it.

It was a strange statue. A statue of a person. Its arms were broken off, and its body protruded above the ground from the waist. It was rather large, and its head, eyes, and ears were all perfect.

I looked closely at the statue, which must have been the statue of an ancient Roman nobleman. It was clear that they had been afraid that the trunk of the body would break if they tried to take it out of the ground, so they had left it there for the time being. It might have been the statue of a god.

I immediately asked Mr. Night: "Mr. Night, I wonder if this is the statue of a Roman nobleman?"

Mr. Night said: "No—well, actually I don't know. It's not the statue of a nobleman; it might be the statue of a god. But don't worry about whose statue it is right now, just look where the statue is looking. See, we're four hundred meters away from Orpheus' house again. We and the statue are all looking at the house."

Just then my brain started firing like a jet engine. That meant there was always someone looking at Orpheus' house.

I looked where the statue was looking. Far ahead of us, I could see the shadow that must be Orpheus' house. It seemed as though there was a light burning somewhere in the upper story. This was a light we had not seen before.

Suddenly, it seemed as if a hot wind blew past me.

Mr. Night stood next to me, squinting, looking carefully at the house in the darkness. I was looking too, but I couldn't see anything yet.

Mr. Night said: "The Alfa Romeo is parked where it was yesterday. There's no movement in the house right now. Wait, wait, someone's coming out into the garden; now he's gone back inside again. Strange, I think Orpheus is alone again."

He kept on looking at the house. It was as though Orpheus' house fascinated Mr. Night as much as it fascinated me.

I kept thinking of something.

"Mr. Night," I said. "You know what I was thinking? We actually can only really see very little ... You see something, but I can't see anything. But this statue of the god is here day and night, so it must see lots of things. Do you think it has something to do with Orpheus?"

I was leaning against the statue as I said this. Mr. Night wasn't even listening to me. All his attention was on the house.

Suddenly: "There ... there, I see him again—Orpheus. He's come outside, and he's sitting there again."

Mr. Night was getting more and more excited.

It was as though he had put his eyes up to the invisible binoculars again and was looking and giving me information.

"He's gone inside again. He must be a very restless person."

The light games of the night before began again in the house. First the lights in the garden went out and came back on again, and then the lights began to flash on and off all over this house that seemed like a space house.

I began to feel very frightened and agitated.

Mr. Night: "He's sensed you. It's as though he's sensed your presence again ... There are very unusual things going on in the house tonight ... It's almost as if someone were going crazy in the house," he said.

I thought of something.

"What day of the month is it, Mr. Night?" I asked. At the same time I was looking at my wristwatch.

Mr. Night answered me without removing his eyes from the house: "Today is the 12th of August. The hour, wait a minute," he said, looking at his own watch. "It's 11:20 right now. Do you see the lights? He's wandering around inside the house again."

Yes, I was following the lights. There seemed to be an earthquake going on inside this house that was like a space house.

Suddenly all the lights went out.

This upset me even more.

The house was now buried in darkness.

How was Orpheus able to turn the lights on and off instantaneously in this shadow that resembled a huge house?

The sudden plunging of the house into complete darkness upset me, as I have said before.

My assistant said: "Look, I've thought of something. Maybe he saw us and he's observing us from some spot in the darkness."

"But why should Orpheus do such a thing," I asked my assistant. "I mean, why should he watch us?"

"Why not?" said my assistant. "Orpheus has no idea who I am. If he saw you, then he would certainly wonder who I am. He knows as little about us as we know about him. He might be curious.

"And tell me, does he know that you're here in this shore city?" he asked.

"I imagine he doesn't know. How could he know? I only just got here. I never go out of my hotel during the daytime," I said.

"It's a strange thing, but he seems to sense somehow that you're here," my assistant said. We sat on either side of the statue. In the darkness of the night, the statue was looking straight ahead towards Orpheus' house.

The house was pitch black. There was not the slightest glimmer of light seeping out from anywhere.

"He's probably asleep," I said.

"So quickly? How can anybody who was driving us all crazy with those lights a minute ago be asleep already? I don't think so. My guess is that he's somewhere in the darkness right now …

"I forgot to ask you. Are his eyes strong?" my assistant inquired.

"I think his eyes are quite strong. Come on, let's go, Mr. Night," I said insistently to my assistant.

We slowly began to walk away among the huge stones.

Something we had never expected occurred at that moment.

The Alfa Romeo suddenly lit up!

But we had heard nothing, no noise of someone getting into the car, or the door opening, I don't know, no noise at all.

The Alfa Romeo's high beams lit up the whole road.

"My God, he's not going, is he?" I shouted out impulsively.

We had crouched down and were watching the car.

The person at the wheel—we couldn't see him—turned off the high beams and turned on the low beams.

There was no light inside the car.

Then he started the engine.

We heard a great roar.

The rumbling reached out as far as where we were standing and echoed against the stones.

Both Mr. Night and I trembled.

Suddenly all the activity in the car stopped.

The lights went out.

The motor died.

The door opened, and a shadow got out of the car. He slammed the car door, then entered the house from someplace we couldn't see.

My assistant and I were frozen, staring into the darkness.

A light went on in the upper floor, then went out.

The whole house was dark again.

"He decided to go—then he changed his mind—I wouldn't want to be in his place. There's a terrible storm going on inside him," my assistant said.

At that point, the car, the house, everything was pitch black.

"Let's get out of here," I said.

We walked back to the hotel, stumbling over the rocks.

It kept getting warmer.

"I think it will be quite hot tomorrow. It would be better if you didn't stay out in the sun too much during the day. Don't go out of your hotel … You've had a big shock tonight …

"The car's suddenly coming to life, and then stopping …

"Well, we shouldn't think about this too much tonight. I'll come to your hotel tomorrow night at eight. Get a good rest," said my assistant.

We said goodbye.

I went into the hotel. Everyone was asleep. I took my key from the key rack and went up to my room.

My shoes were covered with dust. I put them out on the balcony. I walked back and forth in the room for a while.

It was hard for me to sleep that night.

The heat woke me up in the morning. I had forgotten to draw the curtain when I went to bed. The sun was shining on me where I lay. I woke up covered with sweat.

I was like a sleepwalker.

If I had some tea, maybe I could pull myself together a little.

I rang the bell. A little later, the bellboy came.

"Good morning, ma'am," he said.

He had an envelope in his hand.

"A message came for you. Early this morning. By carrier pigeon. I waited for you to wake up. Here's your letter," he said.

He held out the letter.

Even in my sleepy condition I was astonished.

"This letter came by carrier pigeon?" I asked.

"Yes, ma'am. A carrier pigeon brought it. I was very excited too. Because we've never had a guest get news by carrier pigeon before. I know it's none of my business, but could I ask, do you use this mode of communicating a lot?" he asked.

I liked this kid, he was a sweetheart. He was full of life—wanted to learn everything.

"Yes, you can get messages by carrier pigeon. But it's a mode of communication that isn't used very much these days ... Well, anyway, would you please bring me two glasses of strong tea," I said.

The bellboy said: "I'll bring you your tea right away. Your room will be cleaned and the sheets changed today. Do you need anything else?"

"No, that's all for now, thanks," I said.

The bellboy ran downstairs to get my tea.

After he left I looked at the envelope in my hand. The envelope brought to my hotel in the shore city in the morning by carrier pigeon ...

I was no longer sleepy.

There was a faint lilac-colored line drawn along the edge of the envelope, and I noticed a seal that I hadn't seen before. Only the name of my hotel and my room number were written on the envelope.

I went out on the balcony and looked closely at the seal.

It was a gold seal, with a mysterious figure on it!

I broke it and opened the envelope.

The letter, in an incredible handwriting, started like this.

Dear Eurydice,

You were very close to me yesterday. I hope you aren't surprised at receiving this letter. I dictated it to the morning breeze and sent it with a carrier pigeon.

Orpheus

I have involuntarily witnessed some disappointments, childish joys, and difficult situations that you have experienced.

At one point you almost recognized me.

Yes, I am the statue half-buried in the earth of the archaeological site on the hill, the one with the broken arms.

I would like to help you, because all year long I just stand there and stare at the same spot. Yes, I stare at Orpheus' house.

I have to look at it. I look at it whether I want to or not. I can't turn my head even if I want to. A statue can't move. You know that ...

Besides, many of the things you said and did with your assistant interested me. If you like, we could communicate by means of the carrier pigeon.

Believe me, last night your warmth brought me to life.

Loneliness has grown around me from the stone and the earth, from the weather and the passage of time.

Please don't be frightened ... You have one more friend in this shore city.

Respectfully,
Hadrian,
Emperor of Rome

I stood there frozen with the letter in my hand.

Yes, if it hadn't been so dark last night I would have recognized the Roman Emperor Hadrian.

What a deeply personal letter this lonely statue had written to me.

The great Roman Emperor Hadrian.

I was touched, and I sat there on my bed holding the letter. Someone rapped at the door.

"Come in," I said.

The bellboy had brought two glasses of tea on a tray.

I stared at him, my cigarette in my hand. He was waiting to see if I wanted anything.

"I was going to tell you ... If that carrier pigeon comes back again, catch it, so I can answer the message I got," I said.

The bellboy said: "Oh ma'am, I was going to tell you. The pigeon came, it's downstairs."

"Fine," I said to the boy. "Keep the pigeon downstairs. I'll be down in the lobby in a few minutes with a response."

"Yes, ma'am," said the bellboy.

He bowed and left.

I walked around in my room for a minute. The Roman Emperor Hadrian must want an answer from me very badly if he sent the carrier pigeon back this soon.

I rooted around in my bag and pulled out my special stationery and envelopes.

I went out to the table on the balcony, pulled a chair under me, and started to write:

Dear Emperor Hadrian,

I received your kind letter just now. I was touched by your sentiments. First of all, I would like to thank you for your interest. I had just finished reading your letter when I learned that the carrier pigeon was waiting downstairs. I am writing back to you immediately.

I am so pleased that the strange things which took place last night, my childish reactions, and my happiness gave you vitality.

I have strange roots myself and, believe me, sometimes I am incapable of moving from where I am. So you mustn't let yourself get depressed about being buried up to the waist in the ground, as you wrote in your letter.

As far as your arms are concerned, dear Emperor, at this point in time my arms are broken as well. But in any event you quite accurately noticed this last night. You saw right away that I was struggling, and that I was helpless at certain moments!

You say, "All year long I stand there and stare at the same spot." Dear Hadrian, aren't most of us like that? Don't most of us just stare at the same things all our lives?

Again, thank you for your interest.

Yes, I'd like to correspond with you.

I think I'll be coming there tonight with my assistant. Let's see what happens.

There's one more interesting thing, Dear Emperor. You know death. Because you have lived it. But I don't know it yet. Perhaps you can enlighten me on this subject.

Respectfully,
E.

I quickly looked over the letter. Actually, I didn't know how to write a letter to an emperor. I had never written one before.

The Emperor Hadrian had really written to me from the heart.

Leaving my door ajar so that the room would air out, I ran downstairs.

The carrier pigeon was quietly waiting there in the lobby, next to the bellboy. It had a golden chain on its left foot and a ring for attaching the letter. I gently took the carrier pigeon into my hand and slipped the letter into the ring.

I went to the door of the hotel, and I released the pigeon.

It flapped its wings once or twice, then took off like an arrow for the hill. While all of this was going on in the lobby, the only other person there was the bellboy standing next to me.

He considered the whole idea of a carrier pigeon to be perfectly ordinary by now.

"I've never seen this system used before, ma'am. Really, you know I'd never seen anybody use a mode of communication like this. The guests who come here almost always just put a stamp or two on the envelopes and put their letters in the mailbox. This is great; it's so different. I wonder, how long does it take the carrier pigeon to get to where he's going?" he asked.

"I think it'll get there very quickly. When it comes back again, grab it and bring word to me upstairs right away," I said to the bellboy.

"Of course, ma'am, I'll tell you right away," said the bellboy.

I was just about to go upstairs when the bellboy said, "Ma'am, your room is being cleaned."

"In that case, bring me another tea to that table over in the corner, and a light breakfast too. I don't want eggs," I said.

I went and sat down at the table in the corner. The boy had gone to the kitchen.

As I sat there, I thought of what I knew about the Emperor Hadrian.

What I remembered was this: Hadrian was born in 76 A.D. in Rome. He was emperor between 117 and 138. He was the adopted son of Trajan. He took the throne after Trajan's death. He was famous for his extreme fondness for art and literature. He built many temples and villas in Rome and in Ephesus.

I reflected on all of this.

In other words, Emperor Hadrian was already a mature person when he ascended to the throne.

I suddenly thought of something.

No doubt the Emperor Hadrian knew many things and had seen many things both during his life and in his time as a lonely statue in that shore city.

But they might smuggle the statue out of the shore city at any time. It was this thought that upset me so. The more I thought, the more confused I became. How could they leave such a valuable statue alone up there on top of the hill in the archaeological site? Two people could easily break him off at the waist and carry him away from this shore city.

How well was the archaeological site protected?

I was annoyed with myself for not having asked these things in the letter I wrote to Emperor Hadrian. I thought some more. Was Emperor Hadrian aware of the danger he was in, I wondered? Perhaps I would have to get in touch with the museum officials and ask some questions.

I needed to let my assistant know all about these new thoughts in which I had gotten so caught up.

I ate half my breakfast, a little jam, cheese, and honey. Then I went back to the corner. I dialed Mr. Night's number.

He answered on the second ring, as usual.

"Good morning," I said when I heard his voice.

"Good morning," said my assistant on the other end. "How are you; I hope you had a pleasant night."

I said slowly: "Mr. Night. After you dropped me off at my hotel last night such unbelievable things happened that I thought I'd better let you know right away."

From the other end, my assistant asked excitedly: "With regard to Orpheus?"

"Not exactly," I said. "But you could say they're more or less connected."

"I understand," said my assistant. "They must be related to Ankara. Because I got the news this morning that there was a big new avenue being laid out in the new development on the shore. All the young people are talking about two new beer and hamburger places on this avenue — 'Bimbo Hamburger' and 'Escale.' The new development has brought a lot of new people along with it too. As far as I can figure out, Ankara is quickly settling in and developing right next to us.

"You've probably heard something about the city moving in too," he said.

Orpheus

"No," I said to my assistant. "I haven't heard anything about it at all. I was going to tell you about something entirely different. Last night, in that archaeological site, there was a statue from the ancient Roman period with its arms broken, remember? Well, it was a statue of Emperor Hadrian. He heard our conversation and sent a letter to me this morning by a special carrier pigeon. After the pigeon brought the letter, it flew around here a little bit and then came into the lobby again. At the same time, I got an answer ready and was waiting for the pigeon. My letter must have got to Emperor Hadrian by now ..."

On the other end of the telephone, my assistant was quite astonished.

"So, that was the Roman Emperor Hadrian, that statue half-buried in the earth, who stares continuously at Orpheus' house ... you mean he began to communicate with you this morning? That's really incredible," he said.

I said to my assistant: "Tonight we'll look at the house from next to the Emperor. In the letter I sent with the carrier pigeon, I wrote to the Emperor that we would come there tonight. He's waiting for us now. I think the Emperor has seen many things. But just now it occurred to me that they could smuggle him away from where he is now to the islands across the way. Mr. Night, what do you think about this? How well is that archaeological site protected, I wonder?"

It was clear that my assistant was in thought on the other end of the phone ...

"Believe me, I didn't know that statue was of Emperor Hadrian. What you said is true. It must be a very valuable statue. I didn't think of what it meant to leave it there at a time like this, when there's so much smuggling of antiquities. Do you think I should talk to the museum authorities today?" he asked.

I thought for a moment.

"Wait," I said. "I don't want anything to happen to Hadrian. If you ask me, let's not attract the attention of the museum. Besides, Emperor Hadrian seemed to be happy where he was. He'll experience and observe things together with us. He's used to the open air, the wind, the clouds, the day and the night. He might be bored in the museum.

"He wrote in the letter that he knows Orpheus' house very well.

"I've only been here for these few days, and I'm taking responsibility for the statue. I'm pleased that he knows certain things, that he's becoming happy and involved in life. So, come to my hotel tonight at eight. We'll go the same way we went last night to the site where the Emperor is, and this time the three of us will look at Orpheus' house," I said.

My assistant asked: "Can Emperor Hadrian talk?"

"No," I said. "He can only hear what's being said, and see; then he communicates by letter."

"I'll be at your hotel at eight this evening. Goodbye for now," said my assistant.

I said goodbye and hung up the telephone.

The bellboy appeared in the corner with towels in his hand. "Your room is ready, ma'am. I was just bringing your clean towels upstairs."

"Fine. I was going to go outside and walk around a little. You can put the towels in the bathroom. But don't forget, if the carrier pigeon comes, make sure he waits for me," I said.

"Yes, ma'am," he said.

I went out into the mid-day heat. I was leaving the hotel at this hour for the first time. It was unbearably hot in the dusty streets.

I turned off the main street and began to walk along a street I didn't know at all. It was so hot that even the locals of the shore city were nowhere to be seen.

I have to get myself a hat, I thought. My clothes were sticking to my skin with sweat. I walked along one of the streets of the shore city in the noon heat, without knowing where I was going.

Where did Orpheus' house lie? On which side was Emperor Hadrian's statue? By daylight, it seemed, I couldn't locate them at all.

It occurred to me that I should get back to my hotel. I shouldn't walk around outside in the heat.

There was a burning wind coming from the sea. For some reason I had gone out at exactly the wrong time. The intense events of the morning had excited me.

I walked farther along, lost in thought, following the line of the shore. The sun was too strong for my eyes; I rooted around in my bag, found my sunglasses, and put them on. Even in my purse, the glasses were hot. They were plain sunglasses, made from plastic. But at least they shielded my weak eyes from the burning sun.

The first chance I got, I had to find a pharmacy and get myself some good sunglasses.

It was clear that I was getting farther and farther away from the city center.

There were no shops nearby. Only houses here and there, with all their shutters closed at this hour.

At that moment I heard a strange, powerful metallic voice coming from a distance.

At first I couldn't figure out what the voice was, what it was saying. I stopped in the middle of the street and listened.

I understood.

A police car was talking through its microphone. I realized that a policeman was saying something on his microphone from inside a squad car that I couldn't see.

"06 NZ 963, please pull over to the right! 06 NZ 963, please pull over to the right. You're stopping traffic," it was saying.

I must have been a little dazed from the heat, because I went over to the right side of the road and stopped.

A laugh went out over the microphone. Then I recognized the voice. It was Ankara's voice!

Where was the microphone? Where was she calling from? I couldn't figure it out.

Ankara was laughing crazily at me with her smoky voice over the microphone, hiding in some place I couldn't see.

"Yeah," she said, "When you heard 06 (Ankara), you just pulled over to the right, didn't you? What are you, a car? You're kidding, aren't you?

"See how well-programmed you are for my streets."

The city of the plains was laughing away. I realized I must be very close to her.

She spoke with that thick voice of hers again: "How are you? How are you?" she asked.

"Ankara, where are you? Is this any kind of joke to play on a friend?" I said.

"Shout, shout a little, I can't quite hear you," she rumbled out from the microphone.

So I yelled, although I was laughing at the same time.

"Can you hear me now? Is this any way to act?" I said.

She let out another shriek of laughter.

"Honey, friends play these kinds of jokes on one another—and anyway, how did you find your way here in this hellish heat, with nobody else around? And what are you looking for outside in this heat? You usually don't go out at this time of day … Where did you find those ridiculous sunglasses? Are they toy glasses? Do you realize that you're covered with sweat? You're going to have sunstroke, and you have no idea …"

Ankara was talking like an affectionate mother.

"Ankara, where are you? Where are you setting up the seaside development? I can't see you, how can you see me? I can't see the development you've set up from here either. I can hear that you've brought a police car along with you, though," I said.

She was still laughing away.

"We're over behind that hill. I still haven't built the seaside development. I'm working on Tunali Hilmi Avenue. Just let me settle in, and then I'm expecting you to visit. But go back to your hotel for now. It's getting hot," she said.

"I'm going back. I'm going back. Anyway, my whole body is covered with sweat," I said.

"I'll call you in the hotel," said Ankara.

I waved my hand at the city behind the hill, the city that I still hadn't seen, but that was quickly settling in.

I went back to my hotel the way I had come.

I saw the bellboy in the lobby.

"A Pepsi in my room, please," I said.

"Yes, ma'am. You shouldn't go out in this heat," he said.

I thought of something.

"Has anyone called me?" I asked. The bellboy took bottles of Pepsi out of the case.

"No ma'am, no one called you while you were out. I was here all the time," he said.

I took my keys and the Pepsi and went up to the second floor.

I sat on my bed. I drank the Pepsi. I was drenched in sweat.

I was going to meet with Mr. Night a little while later.

"You're sunburned," said my assistant.

"Yes, I walked around a lot this afternoon."

Right there I calmly told my assistant how I had walked around in the hot streets and about the joke Ankara had played on me.

He laughed a lot too at the trick Ankara had played.

"It must be a very coquettish, clever city, this Ankara," he said.

We left the hotel and started to walk in the night.

Mr. Night said: "Look, I've thought of something. Do you think it's right for you to be walking around in the middle of the day, on streets you don't know? You know, you're in danger too ..."

"Oh Mr. Night," I said. "You're talking about death, aren't you? You know, I didn't even think of it. And death is everywhere, all the time. And besides, I don't think of him as being a figure, a person involved in all of these things, do you?"

Mr. Night was thoughtful.

"I really have no idea. But for you to go out like that and wander around all by yourself when there's no one around doesn't strike me as a good idea. I realize that you've rested now. You're bored with staying in the hotel all day long. But still, listen to me. Going out in that oppressive heat is not right at all. You're still not really used to the climate in this shore city," he said.

He quickened his steps slightly.

We turned off the main road and began to walk up the hill the way we had the day before.

A star-filled night had begun once more. There was a hot wind blowing, but it wasn't unpleasant at all.

A little later, we stopped and sat on a stone wall along the way to have a cigarette.

I thought of a question and asked, "Have you ever seen Ankara? I don't think you've ever been around there," I said.

My assistant: "Would you believe, I've never been to Ankara. But I know Izmir very well. I've spent a major part of my life in this shore city."

I turned and looked at him with interest.

In other words, Mr. Night had another universe ...

I smiled. "Just let Ankara get settled in here, and I'll show you around Tunali Hilmi. There's a new mall that's opened there. I think Ankara brought that mall with all its shops here too.

"I'll show you some shops I know. There are booksellers there; I'll take you to them," I said.

Mr. Night: "Did you say mall? What kind of mall is it?"

"Not bad," I said. "It's livened up Tunali Hilmi Avenue. It has three stories with a lot of shops. There are escalators. In the winter I would get warm inside; I don't know what it's like in the summer. But anyhow, it would be a change."

"Has Ankara brought all this with it?" my assistant asked.

"I think she brought it. Let's wait and see," I said.

We started to walk again. A little while later I realized that we had entered the archaeological site. We were walking among the stones again.

Again, I lost my sense of direction.

"Are we going to look at the statue and Orpheus' house from a different angle tonight, Mr. Night? It seems that we come here a different way every night..." I said.

My assistant laughed.

"Look again, we came the way we came last night," he said. I looked in the direction in which he had pointed.

I immediately drew back.

"Oh Mr. Night, there's someone there! Someone is looking at us," I whispered.

Mr. Night was calm.

"That's Emperor Hadrian's statue, come on," he said.

Five minutes later we were beside the statue.

This time I looked rather carefully and saw how magnificent and how lonely this statue of the Emperor was, half-buried in the earth.

At that moment the Emperor was listening to us and following what was going on.

I looked at his eyes, which were staring at eternity.

He was looking, as always, at Orpheus' house.

The house was completely dark tonight.

I turned towards the statue of the Emperor: "Emperor Hadrian, you see that we have come as I promised ... I hope the carrier pigeon delivered my letter to you ... Let me introduce you to my assistant, Mr. Night.

"Mr. Night—Emperor Hadrian," I said.

Mr. Night leaned towards the statue of Emperor Hadrian and saluted it.

Emperor Hadrian's statue remained completely motionless in the darkness.

As there was someone with us who was incapable of speech, Mr. Night and I began to speak all the more.

Orpheus

"How was your day, Hadrian, sir?" I asked.

There was no answer to my question.

I continued my conversation: "If you have no objection, my assistant will sit on your right, and I on your left. As you know, the path here was very tiring. Let's take a seat and see what's going to happen tonight," I said.

My assistant and I sat on either side of the statue.

The three of us were looking at Orpheus' house in the darkness.

At one point my assistant turned to me: "What a pity that there's a while until the full moon. We can't see the Emperor's face clearly," he whispered in my ear.

Then I whispered into my assistant's ear: "Oh Mr. Night, I think the Emperor's hearing is very strong … He heard what you said, and what I'm saying right now."

Then I slowly touched the stone shoulder of Emperor Hadrian.

"Hadrian, sir, are you listening? Please forgive us, because we don't know how people should talk when they're with an emperor," I said.

Mr. Night: "Hadrian, sir, I looked at a lot of books in the library in the city today and learned many things about you. For example, I saw the plans of your villas in Ephesus and Rome. They were really beautiful," he said.

Then I broke in: "Hadrian, sir, you're a person who's built so many beautiful temples and villas. Your fondness for fine arts is well known to every student of history and archaeology. Something just occurred to me! What do you think of Orpheus' house? It's built in a rather unique architectural style. There are steps that come all the way down from the perfectly flat roof to the ground. When the lights are on, I feel like I'm looking at a space house. You know, I've never seen the house by daylight. And tonight it's pitch black over there."

The Emperor's statue, as usual, stared into the darkness in endless silence.

I turned to my assistant.

"Mr. Night, it feels like the hot night wind is getting worse. But I like this hilltop very much. I've grown accustomed to it. And in the full moon we'll be able to see everything better."

I turned around to the Emperor's statue again; the darkness was affecting me.

Suddenly I asked, "Hadrian, sir, have you ever heard of a decompression chamber?"

My assistant was astonished that I had turned around and asked such a question, just like that.

He immediately replied for the Emperor Hadrian.

"Why did you think of that now? I know what it is. It's a room like a coffin, locked from the outside, where they put divers who get the bends. It can create the pressure that exists at the water depth where the bends subside; it has valves on the outside, and it's full of dials.

"What made you think of that now?" he asked again.

"I don't know why I thought of it ... I just suddenly thought of a decompression chamber. It's just as if we were in a decompression chamber, even though we're on top of a hill," I said.

My assistant froze for a moment. I felt like I was there with two statues. Then Mr. Night collected himself and said with his customary firm voice, "Why are you so on edge tonight? You're not used to the sun. This hot warm wind that's blowing has affected you. Now let's not talk about things like this anymore, okay?" he said.

I felt a little better and suddenly relaxed.

What my assistant said was right. The sun had affected me. I had come out here in the night and started to talk nonsense to the Emperor.

In order to change the subject, I said: "I imagine you liked the theater very much, Emperor. The Roman theater was very developed in your day. I imagine you saw all the plays from your special box. Still you don't know what movies, television, and video are. But what's the harm? I bet you'd have liked the cinema."

I turned to my assistant.

"Mr. Night, are there any outdoor summer cinemas in this shore city? I'd love to have the Emperor Hadrian see a film and learn what the movies are like," I said.

My assistant was pleased that the topic had changed.

"There are three summer cinemas in the shore city. But how can we carry the Emperor there? These cinemas are down below, in the city center," he said.

"I wonder what films are playing in those cinemas. Do you know, Mr. Night?" I asked.

He thought for a minute. "I think *Last Tango in Paris* is playing in the cinema on the shore," he said.

I was thrilled! I clapped my hands with joy.

"Wonderful! Mr. Hadrian, this is a film by an Italian director that had a great impact. The actors are Marlon Brando and Maria Schneider ... I wonder how we can manage to have you see this film. Let me think ..."

I turned to my assistant.

"But Mr. Night, they censored the film; there's almost nothing left of it," I said.

"We'll have to watch the film first," he said.

Last Tango in Paris!

Without a doubt, the Emperor Hadrian would be intrigued by this film.

Mr. Night and I discussed for some time how we could make this happen.

Life.

Love.

Death.

The film had everything.

At one point my assistant and I moved away from the spot by the statue and continued our discussion.

Was this really the right film to show to an emperor?

"It's quite risqué. I think it would be better if we showed the Emperor an art film ... or a film that shows tourist areas," insisted Mr. Night.

I was not of the same opinion.

"But Mr. Night, this film is playing right now in the shore city. If you ask me, its analysis and message are very interesting. You could even call it psychological ... I think the Emperor would be interested in seeing it. Besides, it's by an Italian director. Let's not forget that he's never seen a film before. The Emperor Hadrian has no idea about the silver screen. How we can show it to him—that's what we really have to figure out," I said.

I didn't want to leave Emperor Hadrian alone for too long. I walked slowly over to the statue.

Mr. Night suddenly touched my arm.

With that slow voice, he said, "Look, look."

I looked where he pointed.

I saw nothing except darkness.

"What is it, what's there, Mr. Night?" I said.

He stared at the same spot without moving his eyes.

"Alfa Romeo ... I hear the Alfa Romeo's rumbling ... listen," he said.

We had come back over to the statue.

I heard it too. The growl of the Alfa Romeo was climbing towards the house in the darkness.

"It's not some other car?" I asked.

He said firmly, "I don't think so."

He was listening.

I was excited again.

I asked, "He's not coming here, is he?"

My assistant laughed.

"No," he said. "Don't forget. This is an archaeological site, even a jeep would have a hard time negotiating these huge stones. And an Alfa Romeo is a sports car."

The car appeared.

It stopped about where it always did, over by Orpheus' house.

In my excitement I drew close to the statue. The blood-hot wind had started up again.

"Mr. Night, can you see? Who's in the car? Who's driving the car?" I asked.

A shiver swept over me like a fever.

Mr. Night was looking at the car.

"Orpheus," he said. "Orpheus has come home."

"What time is it?" I asked.

Mr. Night looked at his watch.

"It's a quarter to eleven," he said.

He didn't move his eyes from the house. At the same time, he was telling me what was going on: "Orpheus went into the house. He locked the car and went into the house. Strange, he didn't turn on a light ... I wonder if he's walking around in the darkness. There's still no light ..."

I was looking at the shadow that was Orpheus' house.

Just then, a dim light turned on somewhere in front of us.

"He lit a light in the front. But the house is dark," said Mr. Night.

Suddenly lights started to go on and off all over Orpheus' house.

I felt very strange inside.

Because of the heat and humidity, it seemed as if the house was moving towards us and then moving father away.

Different-colored lights went on in different places. I saw pale blue, bright yellow, and purple lights go on and off.

Just as I had felt before, the house seemed sometimes so close I could touch it—but just when I was about to reach out and grab it, it would dash away like a flash of light.

Someone walking around quickly in the house was turning on the lights in each room he entered and turning them off in each room he left!

Mr. Night and I had crouched down by the Emperor Hadrian's statue and were watching this light show.

At one point, Mr. Night wiped off the sweat that had collected on his forehead with the back of his hand.

"Strange light plays … like a signal … but I don't think so. Everything we've seen could have been just a coincidence," he said.

I was terrified and trembling.

Everything seemed different tonight.

Orpheus' house, which I had always only seen as a dark shape, seemed to be alive tonight.

The lights went on and off; the house was speaking to us in a language we didn't understand.

"Please, Mr. Night," I said to my assistant. "Your eyes are much better than mine. What do you think these lights mean?"

Mr. Night was leaning forward and squinting, watching the lights.

I looked at the statue of Emperor Hadrian next to us.

He, as always, was staring at the house.

"What time is it, Mr. Night," I asked my assistant.

"Twelve o'clock," he said.

Suddenly all the lights in the house went out.

We waited breathlessly for a moment.

All the lights were out.

I could no longer see the house.

The complete darkness we were staring at now was more terrifying than the lights we had just seen.

There I was at this time of night staring at the endless darkness, with my assistant and the statue of the Emperor buried waist-deep in the earth beside me, the stars above me, and the blood-hot wind all around.

It seemed as though the house had grown much closer to me in the darkness. Orpheus' house appeared to be only fifteen meters away!

I glanced at Mr. Night.

His eyes were fixed on something he was trying to see in the darkness.

The Emperor Hadrian's statue stood there beside us.

I heard a crunching sound.

"Oh Mr. Night," I whispered. "Orpheus. Orpheus is coming, I think."

Mr. Night said calmly: "No, it's not Orpheus. It's some night animal, in the bushes. That's what you heard," he said.

The dark house stayed the same.

I turned to the Emperor's statue.

"Do you know, Emperor, sir, the dark house is very close to me right now?" I said.

The statue seemed covered with sweat. I touched it gently. Maybe the Emperor's statue was damp from the moisture in the air.

Mr. Night said: "There's no motion, no noise, no light. Orpheus must have gone to sleep."

"Maybe," I said. "Let's go."

As though Orpheus were buried in the darkness.

We quietly got up from our places. We both bid farewell to the Emperor Hadrian's statue.

We began to walk again through the archaeological site.

We had gone quite a distance when I twisted my foot on a rock. I staggered, barely able to keep my balance, and clutched at my assistant.

Some force beyond my senses compelled me to bend down and look at the stone.

I knelt down and looked with interest at the stone.

I suddenly realized it was not like the other stones in the archaeological site.

It could be some remnant, more than half buried in the earth.

I nudged my assistant.

"Look, look, Mr. Night," I said. "The stone I just stumbled over seems to be an old relief." My assistant bent down to look at the piece of stone.

"If you ask me, one end of this stone belongs to the other world," he said.

Then he laughed at what he had said.

I was down on the ground, trying to clean away the earth and bits of sand from the stone.

The stone became more distinct each minute.

I turned to my assistant.

"What does that mean, Mr. Night?" I asked. "Do you mean there was some other world that lived beneath this earth?"

I bent down again and continued cleaning around the stone.

Mr. Night: "Who knows, maybe it's still alive ... after all, we're in the middle of an archaeological site," he said.

Suddenly, behind us the night animal howled.

"Look, Mr. Night, look," I said. "Some marks have begun to appear on the stone."

Mr. Night knelt down beside me.

He also began to clean off the sand and earth from the stone with his hands.

The shapes on the stone became clearer.

We both worked at it; the stone seemed as though it were buried in the depths of the earth.

Mr. Night: "The stone, I think, is not just one stone. It must be part of a larger whole. Look at how deeply rooted in the earth it is," he said.

He was tracing the carving on the stone, as though he were seeking the entrance to a labyrinth we would never be able to see.

He suddenly straightened up.

"There are two people in the relief. They're going up a staircase. These must be the steps," he said.

I watched him.

Mr. Night began to scratch away at the earth with the passion of someone solving a half-disclosed mystery.

He had lost all control.

"Mr. Night," I said. "Stop. The place where you're digging could be the door to a Necropolis. Maybe we're at the threshold of an underworld—the city of the dead.

"Stop."

He stood up.

He was sweating.

He was still unsatisfied.

"I'll come back tomorrow and look at the stone in the light," he said.

By the time we got to the hotel it was almost morning.

We were both tense from the series of events we had experienced throughout the night.

At the door, my assistant said: "Dawn will be breaking soon ... You'll sleep easily now. Don't go out of the hotel today. I'll go up at some point and look at the stone relief."

I went up to the second floor with my key in hand and opened the door.

My clothes were covered with thorns, and I hadn't even noticed. My flat-heeled shoes were covered with dust. I took off what I had on. I found my nightgown and put it on.

I sat for a while on my bed. I thought over the strange events of the night.

It really was getting light. Before I got into bed I thought:

The Alfa Romeo's arrival ... Those strange lights coming from the house that looked like a space house, and the darkness ...

The Emperor Hadrian's statue covered with sweat in the hot night wind ...

And *Last Tango in Paris* ...

While I was thinking all this over before I went to sleep, I felt like listening to some calming music.

I went over and got my transistor radio from my bag in the corner and put it next to me.

The novel *Last Tango in Paris* was squeezed somewhere among my clothes.

I got the book out.

I closed the curtains and got ready to go to sleep.

The book was next to me.

I began to play with the station dial on my radio from where I lay.

Suddenly a full, deep male voice from within the radio filled my hotel room.

"AS OF THIS MOMENT THE NEW ADMINISTRATION HAS TAKEN OVER PUBLIC AUTHORITY IN ORDER TO ENSURE INTERNAL AND EXTERNAL SECURITY.

"ALL DEPARTURES FROM AND ARRIVALS IN THE COUNTRY HAVE BEEN HALTED UNTIL FURTHER NOTICE. AS OF THIS MOMENT A 24-HOUR CURFEW IS IN EFFECT."

I jumped from my bed in surprise.

But the voice on the radio was suddenly cut off.

I kept turning the station dial.

But I didn't hear the deep, full male voice from the radio again that night.

I was very tired.

I drifted off …

When I woke up, it was long past noon. My room was unbearably hot, and I was dripping with sweat where I lay. I blinked my eyes and slowly woke up.

I lit a cigarette.

I flipped the dial on the radio next to me.

The radio picked up nothing. A strange static, some unknown interference, filled my ears.

I tried for almost half an hour without finding a single station.

I turned the radio off.

The weather was even hotter today. I took the novel *Last Tango in Paris* off the table next to me. I opened the first page and read:

The film Last Tango in Paris *playing to full houses at every showing demonstrates that the earth is in a period of constant growth. The seasons have taken on a sense of urgency. The snow that begins to fall in November melts and disappears on the first of May. Perhaps the summer will start in the middle of April and end in July? According to people who deal with supernatural events, the acceleration is due to nuclear energy. We are reproducing too. Like an ant heap that has begun to feel the heat.*

The first showing of Last Tango in Paris, *on October 14, 1972, will be known as the beginning of a new period in the cinema.*

In Last Tango in Paris *we see that strange excitement, that hypnotic, primitive force, that disturbing eroticism that motivates mankind. Bertolucci and Brando have created a turning point and successfully achieved a new dimension and understanding for the seventh art.*

Now Last Tango in Paris *has passed into cinema history. It had been years since cinema goers had awaited the opening of a film with so much anticipation and excitement.*

The female lead of Last Tango in Paris, *Maria Schneider, with her mini-skirt and maxi-coat, is one of thousands of young girls who wander around among us. Marlon Brando, wading through the wet streets with his hands in his pockets and his collar raised, is one of the thousands of men going through a crisis, or perhaps all of them.*

What we wait for lasts just a few minutes. Schneider goes in to take a look at an apartment for rent; Brando has already gone in. They meet twice, in the street and in front of a phone booth, then find themselves alone in an empty house.

Brando makes love to the young girl standing up.

The girl's name is Jeanne, the man's, Paul. But they can never learn this. They seek their happiness in each other's existence in an empty house, far removed from every thought and feeling.

It could be the beginning of a new life.

Brando reasserts with this film that he is an actor with the power to carve his name anew in golden letters in the history of the cinema. Maria Schneider, for her part, is advancing with three steps on the road towards becoming a great actress.

The young director Bertolucci, finding such powerful young actors at hand, leaves the dialogue to the needs of the actors and proclaims that he has begun a new age in the universe of the cinema.

I sat up in my bed and thought about the preface I had just read to the novel *Last Tango in Paris.*

I began to turn the dial on the radio at my bedside again.

Suddenly that full, powerful male voice from within the radio was on all the stations.

"THE ADMINISTRATION HAS TAKEN OVER PUBLIC AUTHORITY IN ORDER TO ENSURE INTERNAL AND EXTERNAL SECURITY.

"ALL ENTRIES INTO AND DEPARTURES FROM THE COUNTRY ARE FORBIDDEN UNTIL FURTHER NOTICE.

"AS OF THIS MOMENT A 24-HOUR CURFEW IS IN EFFECT.

"THE ACTIVITIES OF ALL ORGANIZATIONS ARE BANNED UNTIL FURTHER NOTICE."

It was virtually the same announcement I had heard before dawn.

Once again I jumped up from my bed in surprise.

Just as it was in the morning, the voice on the radio was suddenly cut off, leaving endless static in its place.

I went out on the balcony and looked around. In the main street, which I could see from my hotel, people of the shore city wandered around unawares.

Orpheus

Outside my room life was going on; everything was happening as usual.

I stared out for a while.

It had been five or six hours since I heard these announcements.

How was it possible that no one had listened to the radio in all these hours?

I turned to the radio once again. I turned the station dial again and listened.

This time I heard nothing.

The static that had been coming from the radio a little while ago had been cut as well.

I slipped into something, combed my hair, and pressed the bell.

The bellboy came right away.

His face showed no trace of excitement, agitation, or anything else out of the ordinary.

"Good morning," I said. "I'd like tea service in my room."

The bellboy replied: "Right away, ma'am. I've brewed fresh tea. I'll bring it right now. The carrier pigeon brought you a letter early today. You were sleeping, so I didn't bother you. I did as you said and kept the bird downstairs … I gave it a little moistened bread. Here's your letter."

He held out an envelope with lilac stripes on the edges.

I hadn't guessed the Emperor would write a letter and send it with the pigeon this quickly.

I looked at the bellboy again.

He had obviously not heard the radio. I waited for him to leave, then I opened the letter.

The letter read as follows:

Dear Eurydice,

I hope you spent the night comfortably.

I had the blowing south wind write my letter for me very early this morning.

I listened with interest to your questions last night.

After you left me, I listened for a while to your voices coming from far away. You asked your assistant, "Was there another world that lived beneath this world?"

My dear Eurydice, I didn't hear how your assistant answered you, but it is true that there is another world in the depths beneath this earth …

I think you must have come across something while walking. I felt you moving all around in the starlight.

While you are curious about worlds beneath the earth, I, someone who knows them very well (I'm speaking as a statue), am curious about cinema, television, and video.

These must be very secret, unique things.

Surely they're very removed from stone, earth, centuries, and moss.

You spoke about an Italian director.

You said it was a psychological film. What is a film? Please forgive my excitement and curiosity. Because you speak a very different language from the language of the earth that decomposes stones, fossils, and decaying bodies ...

I'm already very anxious to see what I can from this new dimension you've shown me.

It seems that heat, starlight, and the night beast are somehow different.

Hoping to see you tonight.

Respectfully,
Hadrian

I read the letter again.

Opening my bag, I got out my stationery. I started to write to Emperor Hadrian.

Dear Hadrian,

I just received your letter.

Some strange events that I still can't figure out happened last night just before dawn, then again a little while ago. I'd like to ask your opinion.

I think if you know about them, we'll be able to speak about many other things tonight.

First, last night after we left you, we came across a stone with a relief carved on it.

This is not insignificant, Hadrian, sir.

We dug around the stone and uncovered much of it. My assistant determined that there were two human figures on the stone.

If you ask me, this stone could have been at the beginning of the passage Orpheus used to descend to the other world. Tell me, do you know something about all the stones and remains in the archaeological site?

Do you know the plan of the ancient city?

Orpheus

Second, yesterday when I returned to my hotel before dawn, I heard an announcement on the radio at my bedside.

The announcement stated: "THE ADMINISTRATION HAS TAKEN OVER PUBLIC AUTHORITY IN ORDER TO ENSURE INTERNAL AND EXTERNAL SECURITY."

I heard the same announcement on the radio again today. But outside, everything was going on as though it were perfectly normal.

With the hope of discussing these things at greater length under the starlight this evening,

Respectfully,

E.

I sealed the envelope and went down to the reception.

The carrier pigeon was waiting next to the bellboy. He had his head buried under his wing and, with his eyes half open, was watching the people going in and out of the hotel with the dim look of a pigeon.

The bellboy said: "Just like I told you, I gave the bird a lot of damp bread and some wheat I found in the storeroom. He's ready to carry your message."

I tied the message onto the golden ring attached to the pigeon's foot.

I went to the door of the hotel and let the bird go. Opening its wings, it flew straight up towards the hill.

I went up to my room and sat down on the chair on the balcony. Just as I began to think about everything that had happened, there was a tapping at the door.

"Come in," I said.

It was the bellboy.

"Ma'am," he said. "You have a phone call."

"Fine," I said.

Pulling the door closed, I went downstairs.

It had to be Ankara. Who knows what she'd been up to even in this short time, I thought…

I went over to the phone in the corner.

"Yes, hello," I said.

"Hello," Mr. Night replied on the other end. "How are you?"

I was completely taken aback.

His voice was also very excited.

"I found something out that I was going to tell you tonight when I came to the hotel. But I couldn't wait, so I called. I'll be there in a few minutes," he said.

And I said: "Mr. Night, I have very important things to say to you as well. We'll talk when you get here. See you."

We got off the phone.

I could more or less figure out what my assistant was going to tell me when he came.

I went up to my room and put on my low heels and my dark silk jumpsuit. I combed my hair and, taking my cigarettes and matches and my little shoulder bag, locked the door behind me and went down to the reception.

I saw that my assistant had just arrived.

I ran over to him.

There was no one but the two of us in the hotel reception area. I waited in excitement to hear what Mr. Night was going to say.

I saw that he was a little tired and nervous. It was as though he had lost that special aura he always had.

Mr. Night said: "Come on, let's go right now; while we walk along the seaside I'll tell you what I found out today."

We left the hotel and started to walk along the shore.

I looked around me more closely than before. It seemed as though everything was the same as it was every other night. I gave my attention to my assistant.

Mr. Night cleared his throat.

"This morning at dawn, after I left you at the hotel, I went back up to the archaeological site. I found that stone relief. I took a good look at it in the morning light. I wasn't mistaken when I ran my fingers over it during the night. I understood that my hands had felt everything correctly. The relief shows a man and a woman. The man has a string instrument in his hands; they are going up out of a series of etchings that look like steps. As though they were coming out of the underworld.

"As soon as the museum opened, I talked to the official who works there. I asked him for information and told him about the location of the relief and the details of the picture on it.

"The official said they hadn't registered such a stone yet. He added that the numbering of the stones in the excavation hadn't been finished yet.

"When I told the official about the figures on the relief in complete detail, he told me that, based on stories he had heard, these might be images depicting Orpheus and Eurydice.

"The official's a distant relative of mine, so he has no reason to hold back," he said.

My assistant had finished what he had to say.

We were walking and pausing along the seaside.

My assistant was looking very closely at my face.

I was numb.

In other words, there was an artifact showing Orpheus' and my images in that archaeological site.

"Mr. Night, we have to tell Emperor Hadrian right away. Because Emperor Hadrian heard part of what we said when we found the stone last night; he said in the letter he sent this morning that it's true that there is another world in the depths of the earth. And I sent him a letter asking whether he knew the plan of the Old City or not. I also asked whether he knew anything about all the stones and remains in the archaeological site."

This time Mr. Night was listening very carefully to my words.

My assistant said: "You were going to tell me something; that's what you said on the phone ..."

Right then I understood that he had not heard what I heard on the radio.

I didn't say anything.

After we had walked another few steps, I said: "I was going to tell you about the letter Emperor Hadrian sent to me and my response in the morning."

My assistant said: "I'm just about to get my hands on the reels of the film *Last Tango in Paris*. I almost forgot to tell you."

"Fine, great," I said.

My assistant and I melted into the darkness.

We had turned once again onto the rough winding road that led to Orpheus' house.

The night was again as hot as blood.

It seemed as though the number of stars in the sky increased the further up we went away from the shore city.

The sounds of the night insects multiplied.

Mr. Night said: "Let's sit on this wall for a little bit."

We sat on the edge of the wall my assistant had indicated, and we each lit up a cigarette.

The road in front of us was long and confusing.

I asked: "Mr. Night, this road seems longer and stonier than ever before ... We're on the same road, aren't we?"

Mr. Night said: "Till now we've been on the same road. But tonight I'm going to take you to the statue by a different way."

We threw away our cigarettes and set off down the road again.

We walked for a long time.

I suddenly thought of something: "We'll pass by that stone with the relief on it, won't we?" I asked.

"Yes," said Mr. Night. "We're specifically going to go by it."

We were advancing in the darkness.

A little later, I realized we had entered the archaeological site.

My heart began to beat even faster.

A strange wind had sprung up that blew away at least a little of the heat.

The smell of the sea filled my nostrils.

Mr. Night stopped suddenly, as he always did.

"Well, we've come to the stone with the relief on it," he said.

I bent down and looked at the stone closely.

Mr. Night had squatted next to me and was examining the stone.

The change on the relief was obvious enough to attract attention even in the starlight.

I turned to my assistant: "Did you see it?" I asked.

The expression on Mr. Night's face had also changed.

In a slow voice, he said: "Yes, I saw it. Tonight, one of the two figures in the relief is not there," he said.

I began to tremble.

"Which one is not there, Mr. Night. I can't see well in the dark, you know," I said.

My assistant knelt down, feeling the relief with his hands and looking intently.

A little later he got up.

"Believe me, I can't figure out which one is not there. It's unreal. But one of the figures that was on the relief last night and this morning isn't there," he said.

A cold sweat covered my body.

Orpheus

"Orpheus must be missing, Mr. Night," I said. "Since I'm here, next to you, Orpheus must be missing tonight."

I couldn't stay there any longer.

I virtually dragged my assistant along with me as we came to the statue of Emperor Hadrian.

The great statue was standing there as it had for centuries, quiet and motionless.

When I saw it, I relaxed immediately.

I stretched up and looked at his stone eyes looking at eternity.

"Hadrian, sir, here we are. But while coming here we saw a frightening thing. One of the figures on the relief has disappeared!" I said.

Emperor Hadrian looked silently ahead.

I turned and looked to where he always looked.

It was Orpheus' house...

I froze in astonishment.

Orpheus' house, which had looked like an unlit ship every night, was now filled with light.

This image affected me more than anything else.

I turned to my assistant: "Do you see that? Orpheus is in his house. Since he's there, it means that the missing figure must be Eurydice!

"This means I do not exist right now, or death is very close to us."

As we did every night, we sat down on either side of the Emperor's statue and stared as though mesmerized by the house in the distance.

My assistant said: "You can see the house very well tonight, can't you?"

"Yes, it's as though the house were very near to us tonight... If we weren't next to the Emperor's statue, I'd think that we were closer than ever before to the house..." I said.

While the lights were lit, I wanted to look as much as I could into Orpheus' house.

With my eyes as wide open as possible, I sat there next to Mr. Night and the statue, staring straight ahead.

Strangely, nothing was visible in the house that was filled with light.

It was like looking at the sun in the middle of the night.

I turned to my assistant. For a moment, I had trouble even seeing him.

"What do you see, Mr. Night?" I asked.

"Right now I don't see anything," he said.

We sat there, looking at the house which shone brightly like a crystal ball, neither of us able to see a thing in all this brightness.

Our eyes were dazzled.

Mr. Night said: "We got used to seeing in the darkness. We saw so many things in the darkness. Our eyes will get used to the brightness in a little bit. Wait, you'll see."

We looked for a while longer.

The noise of an engine came to us from a distance.

Mr. Night jumped to his feet in excitement.

"The Alfa Romeo! The Alfa Romeo is coming. How strange that we didn't notice in all this brightness that it wasn't parked there in its usual place. It's just now coming … But why is the house all lit up like this? There are things going on tonight we can't understand," he said.

The Alfa Romeo came right behind the house and stopped.

Mr. Night's eyes were on the car.

In a slow voice, he said: "Someone got out of the car. Can you see him? It must be Orpheus, Orpheus …"

I heard the car door close.

I said to Mr. Night: "I couldn't see in the darkness. I didn't see anything in the light either."

Just then a strange thing happened.

All the lights in the house began to go out, room by room.

Mr. Night said: "Yes, it's Orpheus who came … It's dark again."

I stopped.

"Mr. Night," I said. "It seems that he must be observing us just like we're observing him. The way the house went from blazing with lights when he was gone to quietly going dark after he got here was really amazing."

While we watched, the last light in the house went out. Orpheus' house remained the same formless shadow as always.

We stood there for a while.

A little later, some night beast howled from a place behind us.

"Come on, let's go, Mr. Night," I said.

We walked over to where the stone was.

Mr. Night bent over and inspected it again.

"I'm not sure; right now, both figures seem to be here. But I can't be certain," he said.

Orpheus

Since my eyes were very tired I could no longer pick anything out.

"What are you saying, Mr. Night!" I said, and knelt down by the stone.

I felt the stone with my hands in the starlight.

It was utterly confusing.

"I can't figure out anything. Mr. Night, you take another look at it," I said.

Mr. Night traced his hands over the stone with great skill.

At that moment I thought of everything: my twelve-hour bus trip to get to the shore city, my swollen feet, my incredible exhaustion, getting off the bus, my disorientation from the trip, and my arrival at the hotel.

I had found Orpheus.

I was on top of the Old City.

The Roman Emperor Hadrian was now my friend.

His carrier pigeon was carrying my letters.

My assistant had found me in this shore city and was right there with me.

Just across from me in the darkness was Orpheus' house.

I had heard an unclear announcement on the radio.

The City of Ankara had come to the shore city and at that very moment was settling down in some place beyond the ridge.

I didn't know what would happen tomorrow.

Perhaps my whole reality was on that stone, the stone that Mr. Night had touched.

A reality on stone …

This, at the very least, was a description of a grave.

I suddenly put all this out of my mind.

Mr. Night said: "It's unbelievable. There are two figures here now. This time I'm sure."

My assistant began to clear away the earth around the stone a little more.

"There are other shapes coming out underneath—look!" he said.

I knelt down beside him.

Both of us were digging away at the earth underneath Mr. Night's hands.

I was covered with sweat in the blood-hot night.

A little later we uncovered what we wanted.

Mr. Night said: "It's like a diagram; what we found looks something like that."

"Mr. Night, I think we found a plan of the underground city. How well can you see in the darkness? Where are the entrances, I wonder?" I asked.

Mr. Night got down on his knee once again and scrutinized the image we had just unearthed.

"I can't figure it out. If only we had brought a flashlight," he said.

I got my matches out of my bag. We lit a couple of matches and tried to figure out the plan that was carved in the shape of a rectangle on the stone.

Neither of us understood a thing.

Mr. Night said: "I'm going to come again in the morning and look at tnis stone in the daylight. There must be some system to it."

Both of us passed by the statue of Emperor Hadrian deep in thought. We bid him goodbye.

We left the archaeological site; after a long and tiring walk, we arrived at the hotel.

At the door, Mr. Night said: "I'll see you tomorrow night. If I see something really unusual in the morning, I'll call you."

We separated.

I took my keys and went up to my room.

The first thing I did was turn to the radio at my bedside.

I turned on the radio and began to play with the station dial.

There was nothing on any of the stations. After a little while, I turned it off.

I undressed and got into bed.

I thought of the night's events a little.

How strange; neither the bellboy nor Mr. Night had heard the announcement I had heard on the radio. Neither had mentioned it.

I opened the novel *Last Tango in Paris* to a random page and read:

… *Jeanne looked at the corridor onto which a number of rooms opened and began to walk forward. Everything was just as she had left it, as she remembered it. Only the sun had changed its place. Now its orb was illuminating the other wall of the room. In the weak light the cracks on the wall and the water stains looked like a cardiogram illustrating her heartbeat. Jeanne felt the fear and excitement she had experienced that morning all over again …*

I turned away from the wall and pulled up my coverlet over my back. I leafed through the pages of the book and read:

… The entrance of the villa was choked by grass and bushes. The floors were very worn. On top of a little table that stood to one side in the entrance hall there was a brass gas lamp with green glass. The floors were parquet, and the walls were covered with a fabric that had a geometric pattern.

The Algerian had no idea what it meant to stop and rest. The broken, disjointed melodies that came out of his saxophone reminded Paul of the suffering of creatures crushed and ripped apart by their own agonies and screams … From the place where he sat at the head of the table, Paul could see the Algerian stretched out on the divan in the courtyard. The lamp on the table gave out a very dim light …

I drifted off.

When I woke up, I saw that the book had fallen to the floor and all its pages were scattered.

I got up, gathered the pages, and put them by my bedside again.

I turned the station dial on the radio.

I tried every station. I couldn't hear anything but static.

Someone tapped at my door.

It was the bellboy.

"Good morning," I said. "May I have some tea, please."

"Right away, ma'am," he said.

I went out on the balcony and was gazing at a pure white yacht that was just about to anchor in the gleaming blue world under the morning sun. I heard a knock at my door again.

"Come in," I said.

It was the bellboy. It was clear he was out of breath from running up the stairs.

"Ma'am, Ankara is calling you," he said.

He put my tea down on the table.

"I'll be right down," I said.

I took a sip of my tea and went downstairs.

I took the receiver in my hand and said, "Hello."

"Hello," Ankara answered me.

The city of the plains was, as always, full of life.

"So how are you? I put Tunali Hilmi Avenue right by the seaside; but don't come yet ... I'm setting up one of the Number II EGO bus lines from the city. You know, the brick-red ones. I still haven't found just the right place for the Swan Park Mall. You'll die when you see it! The rest is easy. They're going to start the fall clothing sales in a little while. But come before that and have yourself a good look around. I meant to ask how you are—you're okay, aren't you? I'll call you again. For now, bye-bye. Oh, I almost forgot—last night some kids got into trouble in Bimbo Hamburger. It was over a girl, but no big deal. A broken chair, a bloody nose ..." she said.

She hung up the phone.

I went straight up to my room again.

My tea was cold. I drank it in one gulp. I looked out over the balcony. The yacht had anchored.

Someone knocked at my door again.

"Come in," I said.

It was the bellboy again.

"Ma'am, now the carrier pigeon's here. I'm keeping it downstairs like you said; here's your letter," he said.

I took the letter from Emperor Hadrian, broke the seal, opened the envelope, and began to read.

Dear Eurydice,

You were very excited last night. And there were many things that upset you. In the letter you wrote me yesterday morning, you spoke about news from the "radio" ...

What is a radio?

I have everything under control. Please don't worry. All of the forces of nature are acting in harmony.

You must have heard it incorrectly. If what you're talking about is anything like a slave rebellion, I undoubtedly would know about it. Please believe me on this.

Recently the carrier pigeon has only brought me news from you.

Dear Eurydice, as for what really interests you ... I realize that you are very interested in the underground city. I think you've even found its plan on the stone relief. The key to the plan is that it goes from north to south, and diagonally.

Orpheus

On the upper right part of the plan, the first and main entrance to the underground city is indicated by a mark that looks like a star. But there are a number of entrances to the city. I look directly at the easiest entrance, which is in front of me, next to that tree with the thick trunk that's surrounded by bushes.

I know about all the stones and remnants in the archaeological site.

But I don't know about all the changes that have taken place over time, shifts in the earth, earthquakes, the rise and ebb of the sea that once reached up to here, and the changes made by the archaeologists.

The underground city is very confusing, Eurydice. I hope you aren't thinking of going down there.

Last night, after you left, I thought about the film Last Tango in Paris *again, with great interest.*

I hope you come earlier this evening.

Until we meet again.

Respectfully,
Hadrian

I read the letter from the Emperor over again.

Well, Emperor Hadrian had figured out the plan on the relief for us.

I got out my notepaper and began to write a letter to the Emperor on the balcony:

Dear Hadrian,

I just received your letter.

I received in your letter the answer to any number of things that excited, scared, and intrigued me last night in the starlight.

The archaeological site may have undergone many changes since you last saw it. (I have no doubt about your memory of what is in your range of vision.) A large part of the city that lies behind you must now be buried under the earth. I believe the other statues and remains that came out of the archaeological excavation were removed to the museum.

As for the underground city, I think it has managed to preserve itself as a whole without great changes down to the present.

I shall pass on the code you revealed to my assistant shortly.

You ask in your letter what a radio is …

A means for doing what your carrier pigeon does, but much more extensively and easily!

I don't really think I was mistaken about the news on the radio that I wrote to you about. But neither my assistant, nor the bellboy at the hotel, nor even the Capital City had heard about it.

I hope to be able to show you Last Tango in Paris *very soon.*

There will be three of us coming to you tonight.

Until we meet again.

Respectfully,
E.

I folded the letter and placed it in the envelope. I went downstairs. The carrier pigeon was perched behind the bellboy's chair in the kitchen. I took the bird in my hand and placed the letter in the ring on its claw. I went out the door and released it. I looked after it; it circled once over the hotel, found its way, and began to fly towards the top of the hill.

I thought I should call Mr. Night and tell him the latest news.

I dialed the number from the phone in the corner.

As always, he picked up on the second ring.

"Hello," I said.

My assistant recognized my voice: "How are you? How was your night? What's up?" he asked.

"Mr. Night," I said. "Just now, I received a letter from Emperor Hadrian. It was a very illuminating and comforting letter. In it, the Emperor described the entrances to the underground city …"

"What are you saying!" my assistant shouted, losing control of himself.

"Yes," I said. "The way you read the plan is from north to south, and diagonally … The star in the upper right corner of the plan is a sign for the first and main entrance … The Emperor also wrote in his letter that there are a number of ways to get into the city …"

My assistant, on the other end of the telephone, was very excited.

"Impossible … I'm going to bring a flashlight with me tonight. So we weren't wrong after all. What we saw on the relief really was the plan for the underground city. Come down early. I'll be at your hotel at seven o'clock," he said.

We hung up.

I went up to my room; I put sun cream on my arms and shoulders, spread a towel out on the balcony, then lay down on it and started to look through *Last Tango in Paris.*

Orpheus

The sun was too strong for my eyes. I went to find my sunglasses, put them on, and began to turn the pages.

... As the years passed, Jeanne watched with sadness as tall concrete buildings replaced the greenery nearby and as the poor, driven out of the villages, set up their shacks in the area.
"The camera will begin to shoot from above," Tom continued. "Then it will slowly come down straight towards you. As you walk, the camera will come a little closer. At this point there will be music. The camera will close in, close in."
The team went into action and began to move towards the back garden following Jeanne. Jeanne dragged the team behind her through the shrubbery towards a graveyard.

The sun had become quite hot. I closed the book, took off my sunglasses, picked up my towel, and went inside.

As I closed the curtain, I noticed an Ankara number II EGO city bus pass in front of my hotel and disappear around the curve of the hill.

This was the same bus that ran on Tunali Hilmi Avenue in Ankara!

I ran out on the balcony and leaned out, but the bus was long since lost to the eye.

I sat down on my bed and lit up a cigarette. My shoulders, knees, and face began to hurt from the sun. I had rubbed cream all over myself.

I got into the shower and soaped up. I washed my hair. I felt cool and comfortable.

I spent some time letting my hair dry in the sun, then, feeling tired from being in the sun for the first time, I lay down on my bed and rested. I drifted off ...

When I woke up, I had a hard time remembering where I was for a minute. Then, little by little, I remembered everything—my hotel room, the light yellow curtains, the rug on the floor, the shore city outside.

It had gotten late. I would be meeting my assistant in a little while.

I got dressed in a hurry; I straightened out the bed, put on my low-heeled shoes, ran a comb through my hair, got my cigarettes and matches, and went downstairs.

Mr. Night had arrived and was sitting in his spot in the corner.

I went over to him: "How are you? I hope I didn't make you wait too long, Mr. Night. I must have stayed out in the sun too long; after I washed my hair, I went into such a deep sleep that when I woke up I felt like I was in a completely different place ... Even now I feel like I'm sleepwalking," I said.

My assistant stood up.

"I just came myself. I sat down and rested for a minute.

"What you told me this morning kept running through my head all day. I brought along a flashlight," he said.

I suddenly remembered!

"Just one minute, Mr. Night, I'll be right there," I said.

While my assistant watched me in astonishment, I ran up the stairs, got the tiny transistor radio from my bedside, and went downstairs again.

Mr. Night said: "What's that?"

"It's for Emperor Hadrian," I said.

"Interesting, really very interesting ... Emperor Hadrian is probably going to see something like this for the first time," said Mr. Night.

"I imagine so," I said.

My assistant and I had come out of the hotel and were walking along the shore.

Mr. Night was very interested in the entrances to the underground and in the star in the corner of the plan on the stone relief that Hadrian had described in his letter.

All along the way, he kept feeling for the flashlight in his pocket and trying to figure out where the main entrance would be.

A breeze from the sea began to blow straight towards us.

Suddenly a bus turned the corner in front of us and almost ran us over! Mr. Night and I, not knowing what was going on, dashed to the side of the road.

Mr. Night muttered, "That almost got us."

It was the number II EGO bus I had seen that morning. The one that runs on Tunali Hilmi Avenue in Ankara.

I explained to Mr. Night: "That's the new bus Ankara was talking about! She's running it on Tunali Hilmi Avenue, the one she set up on the seaside. I saw it this morning from the balcony. It passed by at the same speed," I said.

Mr. Night was bewildered.

"Well, the capital isn't wasting any time settling down here," he said.

We walked along and came to the corner where we turned every night.

It had long since become dark.

Again, the night was blood-hot. We went into the darkness.

We went by fits and starts along the little goat trails, which twisted and turned like veins.

At one point it seemed to me that the road had changed.

"We're not going on the same road we take every night, Mr. Night?" I asked.

My assistant laughed at my side.

"We're going on the same road. It's a little cloudy tonight, so it seemed like a different road to you. But I am thinking of taking you to the statue on a different road tomorrow ..." he said.

A little later I realized that we had come to the archaeological site.

Climbing over the stones, we came next to the statue of Emperor Hadrian.

Emperor Hadrian, as always, was staring endlessly into space with his marble eyes.

"Hadrian, sir, here we are and I've brought you a radio," I said.

I put my transistor radio down in front of the statue.

Just then I turned and looked behind me.

Orpheus' house was in darkness. There was no light visible.

I quietly leaned down and turned on the radio.

The radio suddenly came to life.

A deep, full male voice spread out across the archaeological site and echoed from all the stones:

We present the news.

Efforts are continuing to assess the damage from the airplane crash near the gulf yesterday. It was announced that, with the death of one more person at the hospital, the death toll has now increased to 30.

The accident took place in the afternoon, and its cause has not yet been determined. In order to investigate whether it was caused by a mechanical failure, a technical team from the plane's manufacturer is expected to arrive in the country this evening ...

For the first time, in an operation performed early this morning in the United States of America, a patient received an artificial kidney. The patient's condition is reported to be good. The artificial kidney has been undergoing experimental tests for three years.

In a bloody coup in Talza, the government of Juan Gomez was overthrown. According to first reports, Prime Minister Juan Gomez, along with the head of state and deputy prime minister, were killed. The situation is now calm. The Juan Gomez government had been in power for three years, after taking over in a bloodless coup.

The world disco dance championship has concluded. England, Luxembourg, and Argentina won the three top places.

In the European Cup, the second games of the first round have been completed, with one exception. The final match is being played at this very moment between the Bayern-Munich and Valencia teams in Munich. Bayern-Munich lost its first match 2-0.

You have been listening to the news.

I was astonished.

The radio had broadcast an ordinary news bulletin and was now playing light music.

I went and turned it down.

I wondered what Emperor Hadrian was thinking after hearing the news.

I looked with great interest at his face carved in stone.

A breeze suddenly seemed to come from nowhere and ruffled our hair.

The statue of Emperor Hadrian looked into eternity in its customary taciturn manner.

I squinted and looked again at Orpheus' house.

There was no light.

Mr. Night, at my side, was ill at ease.

I suppose he was thinking, on the one hand, of the stone relief, and on the other, of the effect on Emperor Hadrian of the news bulletin we had heard.

We were both quiet.

Mr. Night said: "Come, let's take a look at that plan on the stone relief. I have a flashlight. I bet we can see all the details."

I left the radio where it was and followed Mr. Night over to the relief.

At one point I asked, "Mr. Night, why is Orpheus' house without lights?"

"Maybe he's not home yet; maybe he's sleeping ... I don't know myself. What time is it?" he asked.

I looked at my watch in the starlight. It was five past ten.

"It's still very early. We just now heard the ten o'clock news. I can't imagine that Orpheus is asleep at this hour," I said.

The wind that had just started continued to blow and was increasingly growing in force.

A cloud of dust like a huge pipe rose up from the archaeological site and enveloped Mr. Night and myself, hindering us from seeing or walking.

Mr. Night covered his face with his hands: "Cover your face, or your mouth and your eyes will be full of dust," he called to me.

We could hardly hear one another over the moaning of this unusual wind.

I looked behind me; because of the cloud of dust, neither the statue of Emperor Hadrian nor the shape of Orpheus' house was visible.

This wind that had suddenly started to blow terrified me.

My assistant and I were trying, with great effort, to free ourselves from this merciless mass of dust.

Mr. Night said: "What a strange wind, like a hurricane."

Then it became clear that we had turned around in the same place and remained where we had been. We could see the statue of Emperor Hadrian, just in front of us.

"Come, Mr. Night, let's go over to Emperor Hadrian. With all this dust and dirt, we'll hardly be able to see anything more tonight," I said.

When we got over to the Emperor Hadrian, both my assistant and I were ready to drop from exhaustion.

My ears, the roots of my hair, my mouth, and my nose were all full of dust.

I looked at Orpheus' house. My eyes were tearing from the dust.

There was no light in the house.

My assistant and I sank down on either side of the statue.

The wind started to die down.

The light music broadcast on the radio ended. I bent down and turned it off.

It was covered with dust. I blew on it and picked it up.

After my assistant and I had sat there for a while, we saw that there was neither sound nor light around us; we decided to go.

Mr. Night said: "I'm very interested in that plan on the stone relief. You won't believe it, but the dust from that wind just now even got into my pockets. My flashlight is covered with dust—look!" he said, holding out his light.

We said goodbye to Emperor Hadrian and set off down the road. Behind us a night animal howled somewhere.

"Let's go back to the hotel, Mr. Night," I said. "My whole body is filled with a heaviness I can't explain. It must be caused by this strange weather."

Mr. Night said: "We've already turned onto the road back anyway. Believe me, I feel the same way you do. This was a very unusual storm. I've never heard of such a powerful wind blowing around here at this time of year."

We walked on until we got to the hotel. We said goodbye at the door.

My assistant left, after saying: "See you tomorrow night at the same time. Go to bed soon and rest for tonight."

I got my key and went up to my room.

I got undressed and took a shower. I tried to get rid of all the dust and dirt that was all over me.

I lay down on the bed and picked up *Last Tango in Paris*, which was lying on the bed table.

I opened it up at random, as I always did, and began to read.

... The sound of the saxophone coming from the courtyard was now completely different. The Algerian's mood had changed. Something more painful and emotional came now in place of the bright, noisy piece he had been playing ...

Unused furniture was stored in the basement of the hotel. Paul was going to place one or two pieces of wooden furniture, some broken-down old things, in the house in the Rue Jules Vernes as a sign of his presence.

On the top floor, a door was opened and footsteps were heard ...

I put the book down. The wind had picked up again. I got up from my bed to close the balcony door. The sea had whitecaps. All of the boats in the harbor were swaying back and forth with the waves.

I went back to my bed and turned out the light.

I couldn't sleep for a while, then I finally drifted off.

When I woke up in the morning, the sun was beating down on me again.

The weather had cleared up. Everything was sunny and bright.

Orpheus

I put something on, and just as I went out to the balcony to take a look outside, someone rapped on the door.

"Come in," I said.

It was the bellboy.

"Good morning, ma'am," he said. "There was a terrible storm last night. This morning, very early, the carrier pigeon brought you a letter. I didn't come up right away because I figured you were asleep. The carrier pigeon is waiting downstairs. Here's your letter."

I took the envelope he held out. I asked for tea. I went out on the balcony, broke the seal, and opened the letter. I began to read:

Dear Eurydice,

The "radio" brought me great joy, excitement, and astonishment. I had this letter written by the southern hurricane that blew you to pieces last night but comes here very rarely.

When you brought the radio, I imagine you must have anticipated what I might feel after hearing such things as I did. When you brought the radio, you brought me your century and a thousand incomprehensible questions. Don't forget that I am an emperor and live by solving problems. Those I cannot solve, I use my authority to cut, to eradicate.

But this time I have to solve these problems. The results of history have gone beyond my power of authority. All of my actions are limited by this archaeological site and the fact that I'm made out of stone.

The "news" that I heard from the radio revealed to me in all its reality how much the world has grown and how helpless mankind is in the face of this magnitude.

In other words, maps have changed a great deal since my time.

The United States of America is the state of which nation? Where is it, who is its ruler?

As you know, the archaeologists who work on the archaeological site are trying to learn about the remains here and, for example, from my stone trunk, facts related to my century. And I would like to find, see, and evaluate my correlative in this century from this device you call a "radio."

As far as I've already heard, the idea of an empire has changed a lot since my century. But people, after all this time, have still not been able to find a stable system of rule.

And doesn't the "Talza Coup" prove what I've been saying?

And how can it be that competitions take place at the time of such bloody coups?

Dear Eurydice, it's like I'm coming alive by asking these questions.

No one knows better than I the difference between the state of mind of a victorious emperor and that of a defeated one. Believe me, I'm very interested to learn the outcome of the coup in Talza.

I hope you'll be able to enlighten me on the subject of an "artificial kidney."

If possible, please bring the radio tonight. I want to listen to it again.

Does this object that you call a radio broadcast to the world all the time?

Until we meet this evening.

Respectfully,
Hadrian

I read this upsetting letter from the Emperor Hadrian twice.

We had brought this statue whose only occupation is loneliness face to face with our century.

I sat up in bed and lit a cigarette.

I had to write Emperor Hadrian a letter answering all the questions he had asked.

We had moved the Emperor from the archaeological site to the world, to today. We had brought him out from his narrow universe looking at Orpheus' house, from among the ruins, from the stone relief, to a place where he was eye to eye with the terrifying events of our time.

While we thought we were moving Emperor Hadrian a little nearer to our age, hadn't we in fact buried him more deeply in the history of his own earth?

I paced up and down in my room, asking myself these questions.

Then I sat down to write Emperor Hadrian the letter he was waiting for.

Dear Hadrian,

I received your letter just now.

Before I brought you the "radio," I thought about what you would feel. But believe me, not to this extent.

As you pointed out in your letter, by means of the radio, we have exposed you to thousands of questions about our century, and to its terrifying truths.

You are an emperor.

You were a sovereign for years and governed people and nations.

For this reason, I should have realized how deeply you would be affected by the changes in authority.

But I must tell you that there is only one thing that has not changed from your time to ours. And that is a man's lust for power, for which he will stake his entire history, and for which he will pay until the end of his life.

Dear Hadrian, of course the world is much bigger now ...

For example, we listen to a short news bulletin every hour like the one you heard last night at the archaeological site, but we remain completely indifferent to what we hear.

These news items mostly just disappear in the world of our day and in our own problems ...

Yes, the map of the world has greatly changed.

The United States of America is on a newly discovered continent. And right now it is one of the leading nations of the world.

As for the "Talza Coup" that interested you: I don't even know where Talza is! But the reason for this is not that I don't care, but that it's on a very different map from the one you're talking about.

I'll bring you the radio again tonight.

Listening to another news report will help you understand what I've said.

Dear Hadrian, in the different nations of the world there are now more than 4.5 billion people, and many things are happening at every moment.

The thing that interested me in the news you heard last night was the news about the artificial kidney. I too became excited when I heard about it, because it is a very new and special thing.

I hope I was able to enlighten you a little.

See you this evening.

Respectfully,
E.

After I read over the letter once, I put it in an envelope. I went downstairs. The carrier pigeon was by the bellboy, eating grains of millet and wheat.

I tied the letter onto the ring on its ankle and released it from the door of my hotel.

It traced a bow in the air, then flew towards the top of the hill and disappeared.

I went up to my room.

There was still a long time until I would meet with my assistant.

The air was hot, stifling.

I went out on the balcony and tried to think what I would do.

There was no one on the beach.

As always, the inhabitants of the shore city had withdrawn into their houses because of the heat.

I leaned out and looked down from the balcony. The bellboy was watering the geraniums. The branches didn't move. The white yacht anchored in the cove remained there, motionless.

There was really nothing else to do at this hour other than lie down and read.

And the letter Emperor Hadrian had sent was still making me think.

I went over to my bed and picked up *Last Tango in Paris*. I thought I would just open it at random and read something; the things I read had no significance at all. I leafed through the pages and put it down.

I sat there, covered with sweat.

My hand went out to the radio, but suddenly I was afraid to turn it on.

I lit a cigarette. I went out on the balcony again and watched the waves striking the shore.

It seemed like everything was being washed away in front of me: this room, this book, this shore city. Everything was vanishing from before my very eyes. This stifling heat was withering and melting everything.

I was upset, pensive. I had an impulse to pack my bag and go. Then I remembered.

Orpheus!

… At 7:30 I went down to the reception, ready.

I had brought the radio along.

I went and sat down in an armchair in the corner. The heat had not let up. I became lost in thought …

Suddenly I looked, and Mr. Night was standing next to me.

I got up: "How are you, Mr. Night? I was lost in thought sitting there. I didn't see you coming."

Mr. Night was looking at me closely.

"Did something happen?" he asked.

He sat down next to me. I started to tell him.

I told him all about the letter that had come to me from Emperor Hadrian.

He realized how deeply this letter had affected me.

"Did you answer the Emperor's letter?" he asked me.

I said I had answered it, and I told my assistant about the answer I had written.

"I'm taking the radio again tonight, as Emperor Hadrian wants. But Mr. Night, the answers I sent in response to the questions he asked me seem very inadequate. I thought about this all day and couldn't do anything else," I said.

Mr. Night was next to me, listening silently.

"What else could you have written? Don't think about it any more. Look, what do you think we'll see tonight?" he said.

With my assistant next to me, I was a little more relaxed.

"Tonight I think you're going to take me by a very different route, aren't you?" I asked.

"Yes," said Mr. Night.

We left the hotel together and walked along the shore. A little while later, we turned onto that side road that went up to the archaeological site.

At one point I thought of the stone relief. I had completely forgotten about it!

"If we go by this new road, are we going to pass by the stone relief?" I asked.

Mr. Night said: "On the way back, we'll pass right in front of it. I brought my flashlight. After Emperor Hadrian listens to the news bulletin, we'll look at Orpheus' house, and on the way back I'll figure out where the entrance to the underground city is. Anyway, Emperor Hadrian described it to you in his letter ..." he said.

Another thing caught my interest.

"Mr. Night, this means that you know yet another road to Orpheus' house. We're going there from a different direction tonight ..." I said.

"Yes," said Mr. Night.

We continued to walk in the night.

At one point Mr. Night said: "If you'd like, let's sit there on the wall and have a cigarette. We'll have a little break."

I looked at the wall he had indicated and was astonished.

"Isn't this the wall we've sat on every night? Where we sat and had a cigarette?" I asked.

Mr. Night shook his head in the starlight.

"No, absolutely no connection. That wall is on the old road. This is a different wall. If you notice, this one is higher than the other. I might have to help you to sit on this one. First I'll go up on the wall, then I'll pull you up," he said.

I couldn't understand anything.

"Mr. Night," I said. "Isn't it very tiring to climb up such a high wall to rest? We could sit on a different wall."

"No," said Mr. Night. "All of the walls on this road are high like this. I picked out the lowest one so you could climb up. In order to get to Emperor Hadrian's statue, we have to walk a lot more."

My assistant gripped the edge of the wall and pulled himself up. He put his feet on two toeholds and climbed up to the top of the wall.

Mr. Night stood up on top of the wall, which was fairly high. He was majestic. Just then the crescent moon appeared behind him.

"Hand the radio up to me," he said. "Fine, now give me both your hands. Don't be afraid. Place your right foot on the first toehold and your left foot on the one above it. Then I'll pull you right up."

This was a very difficult job for me. I did what my assistant said and managed to get up on the wall, bathed in sweat.

It was a narrow wall; the other side seemed as deep as an abyss to me.

Since I was afraid of heights, I clung to my assistant, trying keep my balance on top of the wall.

Mr. Night said: "Well, you're up. Now let's sit down and each have a cigarette."

He lit up a cigarette; then he lit one for me and handed it to me.

I took a drag on the cigarette and looked out in front.

In front of us in the ink-black night, by the light of the slowly rising crescent moon and the stars, I saw an endless valley stretching out.

The archaeological site, Emperor Hadrian's statue, and another side of Orpheus' house appeared in the far distance.

I was quite excited.

I grabbed Mr. Night's arm: "Do you see? You can see everything from here … We must be very high … otherwise we would never be able to see this view; it's so different, like an old painting," I said.

Mr. Night said: "Yes, we're very high. When we finish our cigarettes, I'll help you. We'll jump down from the wall and get to where the statue is."

I put out my cigarette. Mr. Night flipped his cigarette and threw it into the darkness. Then he leaped off the wall and floated down, as if he were using some invisible parachute.

He called up to me from below.

"Don't be afraid. Press your hands on both sides of the wall, then slowly let your weight down; put your right foot on a toehold on the right, then put your left on a toehold there. I'll hold you."

I did what my assistant said.

With difficulty I got down from the wall. When I got down, I looked, and there was a little scrape on my arm.

We continued to walk in the valley. After walking a while longer, I saw with astonishment that there was another wall in front of us.

This wall was a lot higher than the wall we had already climbed over.

"Mr. Night, I really don't think I'll be able to get over this wall. This new road is really strange. It's as though it has barricades ... What will we do now?" I asked hopelessly.

My assistant said, in a strong voice: "Don't be afraid. I'll show you all the places where you should step. First I'll climb up, then I'll pull you up next to me."

In the light of the crescent moon and stars, he climbed up to the top of the wall like a goat.

He stood up.

"Hold your hands out to me; okay, step there ... give me your right hand ... okay you're up," he said.

This wall was even narrower and older than the first one we had climbed.

"Here's your cigarette," said Mr. Night.

He lit one for himself.

When I got used to the height of the wall, I looked around a little; we were in the archaeological site!

I turned to my assistant.

"Mr. Night, we're only ten meters away from Emperor Hadrian! How strange, how could I have never seen this wall before?" I asked.

Mr. Night said: "We're coming by this road for the first time. In the darkness you can't see this wall from next to Emperor Hadrian's statue."

Emperor Hadrian's statue stood as though waiting for us with its customary mysterious reticence.

Mr. Night slipped down from the wall, again, as though with that invisible parachute.

I came down behind him step by step, out of breath as though descending a steep staircase, and landed by Emperor Hadrian.

This road had really tired me out—tired me, and enchanted me. I was covered with sweat in the hot night.

I had never gone down a road with such tall barricades in my life before.

I went with my assistant over to Emperor Hadrian and we sat down on either side of him.

I looked ahead, at Orpheus' house.

It was completely dark.

Nothing was visible.

I turned to my assistant: "What time is it, Mr. Night?" I asked.

My assistant looked at his watch.

"It's two minutes to ten," he said.

I quickly turned on the radio that was in front of Emperor Hadrian.

The static coming from the radio filled the whole archaeological site.

At first there were conversations going on in languages we didn't know.

I was confused.

I kept playing with the station dial. Suddenly there was a deep, full male voice:

"We present the news," he said.

Preliminary reports indicate that 250 people died and 1,500 were left homeless in the earthquake that occurred early this morning in Sicily. Officials said they fear the death toll will rise and added that efforts continue to clear the wreckage.

The space shuttle Columbia entered its orbit around the earth. According to an announcement by NASA officials, the astronauts have begun previously planned scientific experiments ...

As the investigation connected with the airplane crash of the day before yesterday continues, officials from the plane's manufacturer have avoided providing information about pilot or technical errors. At this point, the black box that can provide all the information has been found and given to the firm's officials ...

Orpheus

The International Peace Commission of the United Nations concluded its work in Brussels on the subject of non-proliferation of nuclear missiles.

The Soviet Union has succeeded, for the first time anywhere, in manufacturing artificial blood. According to a report from the Soviet Union's official TASS news agency, work on artificial blood has been going on for a long time, and experiments in this field have been successfully concluded.

During the filming of a scene in a new film, Roma, *by the famous Italian director Federico Fellini, a curfew was called in the whole city of Rome. In a statement broadcast on television last night, the famous director thanked all the officials and people of Rome for their understanding ...*

A number of agencies report that the situation in Talza is calm. According to a statement from the spokesman of the newly formed government, all international agreements signed by the former government will still be honored ...

Results of the international beauty contest that is taking place in the British capital, London, should be announced shortly ...

In the next 24 hours, the weather will be clear in the coastal regions and partly cloudy with occasional showers in the interior.

You have been listening to the news.

The radio was silent.

The archaeological site suddenly reverberated with static.

I went and shut it off.

Then everything was just as suddenly buried in deep silence.

I looked at Emperor Hadrian's face with great interest.

I wondered what he was thinking?

Emperor Hadrian was staring ahead in silence as always.

I turned and looked.

The house was dark.

A wind as warm as blood rose and fell.

We heard a crunching noise behind us.

My assistant immediately took my arm.

"Please don't be afraid, it's just some night animal," he said.

Both of us stared at the bushes, trying to pick out the night animal.

The noise stopped. It must have been a hedgehog.

Suddenly a giant projector light took us in its scope.

We were blinded by the brightness and stood frozen in our places.

We looked at the brightness but couldn't figure out where it was coming from.

My assistant whispered, "Let's hide behind the statue."

For a minute neither my assistant nor I were able to move from our places. It was as if the huge circle of light had wrapped around our feet like a fish net and enfolded us.

"This must be Orpheus' light!" I said.

My assistant said, "Behind the statue, let's get behind the statue."

It was as if we were running in the sea.

As though we were encircled by the arms of an invisible octopus.

We made a final effort and managed to get behind the statue of Emperor Hadrian.

Both Mr. Night and I were filled with terror.

The light was fixed directly on the statue of Emperor Hadrian.

Without wavering, it illuminated only the statue.

Mr. Night said: "The projector is being directed from Orpheus' house."

"So Orpheus has finally seen us. He's caught us, Mr. Night," I said.

"The two are right across from one another," said Mr. Night. "I don't think he saw us."

For a long time we hid behind the statue in this extraordinary light.

The projector searched the area, the whole archaeological site, and paused.

Then suddenly it went out.

It seemed ten times darker.

I stood there squinting my eyes.

Mr. Night said, "This could be a trick. That huge light could go on again. Let's not go out just yet." We stayed behind the statue a while longer.

Once, I stuck my head out and looked, but I couldn't see anything but darkness.

"Mr. Night," I said. "My heart's going to give out from fear. Let's not stay here anymore. We have to go back to the hotel."

Mr. Night was hesitant.

"What if he catches us on the road with that huge light?" he asked.

We waited a bit longer.

Nature, the darkness, that warm wind blowing—everything was the same.

"Come on," I said.

Very slowly, hiding behind the stones, we made our way out of the archaeological site.

We kept turning and looking back. Orpheus' house was there, without a single light.

We ran back to the hotel.

I was filled with curiosity.

"I wonder if he saw us. We'll never know whether he did. But he obviously knew we were there," I said.

My assistant was very anxious.

"It startled me. Orpheus must be much more powerful than I thought."

We had reached the hotel.

Before we parted, my assistant said: "Rest well tonight. Climbing over those high walls and getting caught by that huge projector have tired you. I'll be at your hotel at the same time tomorrow night."

We said goodbye. I went up to my room.

I was very upset. For a while, I walked purposelessly up and down in my room. I was trying to get rid of at least a little of my inner tension.

I went out on the balcony.

The lights striking the water reminded me of the light of that huge projector. I went back inside.

I lit a cigarette.

I sat there, thinking ... The events of the night—the light that Orpheus had shone on us, the appearance of Emperor Hadrian, and the stones of the archaeological site in that white light ...

I lay down on my bed.

I drifted off ...

In the morning I woke up early. I tossed and turned in my bed for a while. I was still feeling the effects of the night's events.

Then I got up and dressed, and while I was brushing my teeth, there was a rapping on the door.

I spit out into the sink, wiped my mouth, and said, "Come in."

It was the bellboy.

"Good morning, ma'am. I hope I didn't wake you up. The carrier pigeon came just at daybreak. It's eating moistened bread and wheat grain downstairs. Here's your letter," he said.

I took the letter the bellboy held out to me. I broke the seal and opened it.

I began to read with interest the letter Emperor Hadrian had written to me.

Dear Eurydice,

I'm so happy I was able to listen to the radio again last night!

You're right, it seems. Now I better understand what you wanted to explain to me in the letter you sent.

The world really must be much bigger and different now than what I had imagined.

The whole night I tried to interpret and find the connections among the news reports that I've heard over the last two days.

The earthquake in Sicily and the high death toll there saddened me. It's an area I know well …

Then, there was a second piece of news that interested me: when an Italian director with the name of Federico Fellini was filming the movie Roma, *there was a ban on going out into the streets in the whole city of Rome! This event made me very interested in the subject of "films."*

When they were filming the movie Last Tango in Paris *that you spoke of, did something like this happen?*

What is the Soviet Union, and where is it?

Can you tell me something about the artificial blood they made? Isn't there enough blood in the world?

What are the "nuclear missiles" they're trying to limit?

What I really couldn't comprehend, dear Eurydice—in this developed, great world where you have every means and possibility of communication—is why you come every night to stand next to me with your assistant and look from this old (and now I realize just how old) archaeological site, and why you are content to just see the lights in Orpheus' house from a distance of 500 meters?

What do you think of that powerful light that was shone on us from Orpheus' house last night?

The light didn't come on again after you left. And it never happened before either.

This is preoccupying me as much as the "news."

It may just be impossible for me to analyze what happens in the world anymore. But it is possible for me to analyze, judge, and solve what takes place in front of me and what I witness myself.

Until we meet again.

Hadrian

I read the letter from Emperor Hadrian twice carefully.

The Emperor was justifiably asking some questions and seeking answers to them.

I lit a cigarette and walked around my room.

I was in a difficult position.

I almost began to panic.

I wondered, if I called Mr. Night on the phone and told him about the letter and Emperor Hadrian's questions about Orpheus, would he be able to help me?

I didn't even know what I thought myself.

The one thing I knew was that I did not have the strength to remain alone at the hotel until it was time for him to come.

At one point, I was afraid of myself.

Then I opened the door to my room and ran downstairs, went to the phone in the corner, and dialed my assistant's number.

As always, he picked up on the second ring.

Mr. Night said, "Hello."

When I heard his voice, I began to tell him, my words all jumbled up, about the Emperor's letter.

On the other end of the phone, my assistant said: "Stop. Don't get worked up. I'm coming over right now. Your nerves are shot."

I sat down in an armchair near the reception desk.

Just a little later my assistant came running into the hotel.

"How are you? What was it that you said on the phone? Why did you get so panicky?" he asked.

In the heat of the morning, I was covered with sweat.

"Your face is all white," my assistant said.

"I am afraid, Mr. Night," I said. "I am very afraid."

Mr. Night shook his head in wonder.

"I can't understand what you're afraid about," he said.

"Emperor Hadrian's letter scared me, Mr. Night," I said.

He shook his head again.

"Why should Emperor Hadrian's letter scare you? I don't understand.

"Stone, it's just stone … Come on, pull yourself together now," he shouted.

I was paralyzed with astonishment.

Fear made my mouth dry.

"What do you mean by that, Mr. Night?" I asked.

Mr. Night said: "Just what I said … What authority can the statue of an Emperor have? How can it hurt you? I don't understand. I can't figure out why it has this effect, this power over you."

What incomprehensible things my assistant was saying!

I immediately defended the Emperor.

"Mr. Night, how can you talk like that? You know much better than I do that the statue of Emperor Hadrian has seen many things and is powerful and intelligent. His logic is exceptional, his intelligence is extraordinary for our age and time. His memory is excellent … you know the letters from him.

"And besides, we've brought this very old statue into our own century. I feel that responsibility every moment. I thought you felt it too," I said.

Mr. Night said: "All right, but then why were you frightened by Emperor Hadrian's letter?"

"Because it was a letter asking very intelligent questions. It touched on all the major points of what's going on in one fell swoop. That's what scared me a little while ago. Now I'm better," I said.

Mr. Night was looking at me very closely.

"How do you know Emperor Hadrian sent you those letters?" he asked.

I was astonished.

"The Emperor's carrier pigeon brings them. I saw the pigeon downstairs a number of times. I send the letters I write to the Emperor by tying them to the ring on the pigeon's foot," I said.

Mr. Night lit a cigarette.

"Yes, but how do you know that those letters went to Emperor Hadrian?" he asked.

"I just told you," I said.

"In other words?" asked my assistant.

"With Emperor Hadrian's carrier pigeon, Mr. Night," I said.

"Okay," said Mr. Night. "Couldn't this carrier pigeon belong to someone else?"

"Oh, Mr. Night," I laughed. "I don't know anyone else with such extraordinary powers of imagination!"

When I said this, my assistant laughed too.

"Your sense of humor is back. You're okay now." He got up, saying, "After I finish some things I have to do, I'll be at your hotel at the usual hour."

I went up to my room.

The air was now really hot. The letter from Emperor Hadrian was where I had left it on my bed.

I read it again.

I got out my paper and started to write a letter to the Emperor.

Dear Hadrian,

I read your letter over several times.

The question that made me think the most, and that you rightly asked me, concerned Orpheus.

As to why, in this greatly developed and expanded world, with every possibility and means of communication available, I look at Orpheus every night from where you are with my assistant, look from a great distance and am content only to see the lights …

Dear Hadrian, would you believe me, I don't know the reason myself.

A force I cannot describe both draws me towards him and tells me that I have to stay far away from him.

I want to see his presence, his light, because I miss him. But for some reason that I don't know, I'm afraid of him, and I run away.

A strange power is drawing me to him but another power keeps whispering, "Flee! Flee!" into my ear.

Since my eyes don't see well at night, I still haven't seen him.

Judging from my assistant's explanations and making an evaluation from the lights I've seen, I can see that he is also unsettled and looking for something.

I came here knowing these things.

That powerful light that shone on us last night shows that he has sensed our presence as well.

For days I've been living with the distress of a person who doesn't know what to do.

I've found him, but now I don't know what to do next.

Well, let's put all this aside for now and talk about the film Last Tango in Paris.

Maybe when you watch the film you'll be able to find the answers to a lot of your questions, dear Emperor.

My assistant has found a print of the film.

Hoping to show you the film as soon as possible and to see you tonight,

Love,

E.

After I read over the letter I had written to Emperor Hadrian, I folded it and placed it in an envelope.

I went downstairs. The carrier pigeon was next to the bellboy. I took it in my hand and carefully attached the letter to the ring on its claw. I carried the bird out to the door of the hotel and let it loose, just as I did every other time.

I watched after it. It turned in the air, then glided away and was gone.

A breeze scented with iodine blowing from the sea intoxicated me. As I stood there, thinking over the events of last night, I saw the Number II EGO bus approach from afar. It was making good time again, but slowed down near the stop and halted right in front of me.

The front door opened and I got on the bus.

The bus was completely empty. I sat in one of the front seats. We started to head off at top speed towards the hill.

I was excited.

In just a little bit, I would see the Tunali Hilmi Avenue that Ankara had "set up"!

I turned around one last time and looked out the back window of the bus at the hill where Emperor Hadrian's statue, the archaeological site, and Orpheus' house were.

Nothing was visible.

The bus suddenly turned at an intersection.

We had come to the back side of the hill.

In astonishment, I held onto the iron railings in the bus where I sat.

The Number II EGO bus was going down Esat Avenue from Kucukesat, and it turned onto Tunali Hilmi.

I was on Tunali Hilmi!

The bus was heading towards the middle section of the avenue, both sides of which were lined with shops and homes.

There was no sea or anything resembling it in sight.

Orpheus

We had entered into a summer day on Tunali Hilmi Avenue in Ankara.

I got out at the first stop.

The humid air of the seashore had gone, and Ankara's dry heat was in its place!

I slowly began to walk down Tunali Hilmi.

The Avenue was there before me, with all of its characteristics.

The strange thing was that the road going up to Cankaya and the surrounding block apartments were visible from far away.

With the tranquillity of the archaeological site and the sharp, intoxicating iodine smell of the sea lost and gone in this web of noise I had unwittingly entered, Tunali Hilmi's utter confusion completely disoriented me.

For a moment I thought my heart would stop.

I trembled for a moment in this explosion of consciousness.

I turned and looked behind; the Kucukesat intersection and the roads that led down from there to the city completely covered the horizon.

I continued walking.

Beside me, the traffic flowed like a flood.

The sun striking my eyes from the cars, windows, and hoods made me dizzy. The sound of a horn that was stuck kept echoing in my ears.

I squinted.

I thought of looking at my watch. It was 5:30.

I wandered purposelessly down the street, the way I used to do on Sundays. The city was pressing in on me in a strange way.

I went into a shop.

It was a supermarket.

Going past the olive oils, vegetable oils, and sunflower oils in the entry, I came to the section where different kinds of soap, cologne, and toothbrushes were displayed. I continued on into the market. On one side were the sections for different powder and liquid detergents, soft soaps, window wash sprays, candles, and chewing gum; on the other side was a section where sausages, salamis, lamb, mutton and veal, cold cuts, and sweetbreads were arranged.

After passing the different colored candles, I saw colognes, toothpaste and pasta, different kinds of chocolate, chandelier cleaners, and floor polishes, and I noticed more kinds of cookies than I had ever before seen together in one place.

I had a hard time making myself leave the market.

The salesgirls in their blue uniforms looked at me in surprise.

I went out onto Tunali Hilmi again.

The traffic was at a standstill.

I took a handkerchief out of my pocket and wiped away the accumulated sweat from my forehead and neck.

I was like an animal whose leash had been untied.

Like a slave left on her own...

Like an arrow that wanted to return to its bow...

I turned onto a side street, thinking I might be able to escape the city.

But it got even worse; this too was a street that I knew.

It was completely still and had no shade from the summer heat.

I passed in front of buildings that I knew.

Finally, I came out onto Tunali Hilmi again.

I felt like I would drown. The garment I had on was stuck to my back with sweat. The rumble of the city was inside my brain.

I walked up to the end of the road.

I was distressed to see that the road went on.

This time, I came to another intersection. Without thinking, I turned onto one of the roads.

Obviously a summer school was just letting out. A mob of students spread out, shouting in every direction.

I went over to the other sidewalk and started to walk uphill all over again.

I walked on, passing the bookstores and the fish vendors; I turned onto the first side street I came to.

This also was one of those streets I had walked along a thousand times.

It was the street of my shoemaker.

I saw his store in front of me a little further down the street.

Strangely, the shutter was down. Glancing for a second at the window, I passed on.

I began to climb up the hill in front of me; the city was coming over me with all its oppressiveness; I was at the top of Tunali Hilmi again.

This time I began to walk downhill.

Suddenly I saw a familiar face in the crowd.

Orpheus

Hurrying up my steps, I tried to catch up.

Then the person turned, and I saw it was someone I didn't know at all.

I slowed down again, strolling and stopping.

I went back up the sidewalk, trying to escape from this avenue.

Time went on.

Finally, I went over and sat down on a bench.

Tunali seemed to be showing a different face now.

The cucumber seller on the corner had pulled down his hat and was putting salt on his peeled cucumbers. A group of boys and girls had gathered around his stand, talking and laughing. At that point, a full, deep male voice came from the radio above the stand: "We present the news ... As the government crisis caused by the failure to agree on a coalition among the parties reaches its sixty-third day ..."

The cucumber seller reached up and turned off the radio.

Someone who seemed to be up to no good appeared from the opposite corner, wearing a green shirt and yellow pants tucked into white boots with spike heels, with jet-black hair slicked back and a hawk nose. He had his arm through that of his girlfriend and was heatedly explaining something.

They passed in front of me.

I became bored.

I got up and began to walk.

I found the bus stop. I began to wait.

A whole lot of buses going to different areas of Ankara came one after another and passed on.

There was no sign of the Number II bus.

Each bus that passed by seemed to distance me a little more from the shore city.

I just wanted to get away and escape.

I hailed a taxi that was passing along the street.

The taxi slowed down and pulled over to the curb.

I opened the door and got in.

The taxi started.

I said to the driver, "Take the next left."

Leaning back, I looked at the last remains of Tunali Hilmi.

The taxi turned left.

Esat Avenue was lying out there in front of me!

"Left again," I said.

The taxi turned left.

We were on Kennedy Avenue.

"Left again," I said.

We were on Tunali Hilmi.

"Right here," I said.

We came out on Esat Avenue.

"I'll get out here," I said.

I gave the driver his money and got out.

I was covered with sweat.

I got another taxi.

"To the bus terminal," I said.

I leaned back in the seat and lit up a cigarette.

I could no longer think straight.

I had come into Ankara by going over a hill; I would go back to the shore city by a twelve-hour bus ride.

A twelve-hour intersection! Unbelievable!

I got a ticket for a bus leaving for the shore city in half an hour.

From a stand on the corner I got a pack of cigarettes, a package of cookies, and a newspaper for the trip.

I couldn't go into the terminal. Inside me, I had a suspicion I couldn't fathom, a tension I couldn't identify. The noise of the terminal mixed with the voices of the salesmen.

At one point there was a traffic jam.

As the police and soldiers with guns in their hands lined themselves up on either side of the road, a jeep with a blue spotlight on top passed quickly in front of us.

Behind it, jet-black cars appeared. They drove up the hill one after another.

Just then I saw the Number II EGO bus in the traffic jam.

I began to run.

I passed behind the cars and got to the front door of the bus.

The driver was following the disappearing convoy with great indifference.

I began to pound on the door.

The bus was completely empty.

The door opened.

I jumped on board.

The traffic went back to normal.

The bus began to advance.

The road was narrowing.

The bus seemed to speed up.

The driver suddenly braked. The things I had gotten from the stand fell off my lap and scattered all over the floor.

It was as though the exhaustion of a twelve-hour trip had suddenly dissipated.

I bent down and started to pick up the things that had fallen.

As I was gathering up the cookies, the package of cigarettes, and the newspaper, a sharp smell of iodine came to my nostrils.

I straightened up and looked.

The bus was swaying around a hill.

Turning, I looked out the back window of the bus.

Nothing was visible because of the dust.

I jumped out of my seat.

The shore city was in front of me!

The bus stopped in front of my hotel.

When I got off, the bellboy was watering the geraniums.

I went straight up to my room.

I took off the things I had on and threw myself on the bed.

I looked at my watch.

There was still time before my assistant would come.

I drifted off ...

When I opened my eyes, it was past 7:30.

I jumped up from the bed and quickly got dressed; I combed my hair and ran downstairs.

Mr. Night was sitting in his usual place.

I went over to him: "I think I've made you wait quite a long time, Mr. Night. I was very tired and fell asleep. I went on the Number II EGO bus to Tunali Hilmi today," I said.

Mr. Night was interested: "How is it? Did they do a good job of laying out the new avenue?" he asked.

"Mr. Night," I said. "It's something really unbelievable. That place is not a street ... How can I explain it? It's as though the whole city were there! And once you go in, it's very hard to get out again. It swallows you up like a nightmare. It's very hard to explain ..."

"I didn't understand a thing you said," said Mr. Night. "How could a new street have such an effect on you?"

"I told you; it's not just a street. I can't explain it to you, Mr. Night. It's something unexpected, between seeing and not seeing, like being here and not being here at the same moment ... I don't know, Mr. Night. It's like you're suddenly thinking of yourself being far away. Remember that panic we felt in the archaeological site, and the emptiness you felt the night after you dug up the earth around the stone relief with your fingernails in excitement, and then left everything in the daylight, or even more, something like a car that's moving fast and then suddenly goes into reverse ..." I said.

Mr. Night said: "Well, anyway when you mentioned the car, I thought of something. We'll need a car for that film projector on the tripod that we're going to bring to the archaeological site tomorrow night. I found the reels of the film," he said.

"The car's not important. We'll find one somehow," I said.

My assistant said: "Okay, then, I'll get a car from my relative who works at the museum."

"Please, Mr. Night," I said. "Let's not mix up the museum in this too. As far as I'm concerned, nobody should know what we're going to do."

Mr. Night said: "Don't worry. Nobody's going to know what we're up to."

My assistant and I left the hotel and plunged into the darkness.

We walked on and on and turned onto that twisting road that led up to the archaeological site.

A little while later, my assistant said to me as usual: "If you'd like, we could sit on that wall by the roadside and have a cigarette."

"Tonight we're going by the old road, the one we first came by, aren't we, Mr. Night?" I asked.

"Yes," he said.

We sat on the wall and each lit up a cigarette.

The sky was filled with stars.

A little later, we started off on the road again.

We came into the archaeological site.

Passing among the stones, we headed towards Emperor Hadrian's statue, which could be seen from far away.

I was filled with a childlike joy. I was back here again!

At that moment, I looked at Orpheus' house.

The house was completely dark.

Emperor Hadrian was, as always, staring straight ahead in mighty silence.

Suddenly, Mr. Night grabbed my arm and said in great excitement: "Look, look at that! That huge wall, how did it get knocked down?"

In astonishment, I asked: "What wall?"

Mr. Night ran over to the base of the fallen wall.

I ran after him.

The highest wall we had climbed over with such difficulty only last night had crumbled to pieces.

"Don't get too close!" Mr. Night called out. "The wall is swaying, at any moment another piece could fall off the top."

I drew back.

And stepped on something soft.

I leaned down and looked. I took it in my hand. It was the mail pigeon.

It had died.

It was stiff and cold as ice in my hands.

I called out to my assistant in pain and shock: "Mr. Night, look what happened! A horrible thing. The carrier pigeon is dead!"

Mr. Night ran over to me.

I was holding the pigeon in my hand. I began to tremble all over, uncontrollably.

Mr. Night said: "Wait a minute. Maybe this is a different bird."

"But it has the ring on its ankle that you fasten letters to. This is the one," I said.

Mr. Night was silent.

I couldn't believe the pigeon was dead.

My only means of communication with Emperor Hadrian had been cut!

At that moment the archaeological site seemed to grow larger, infinitely larger. I found myself filled with an inexplicable loneliness.

Now there was no way for us to understand the language of the stones or the language of the centuries.

Mr. Night was surprised as well: "Strange things have happened here," he said.

I had no idea what was going on.

I had run over and was standing next to the statue of Emperor Hadrian.

I looked at him carefully, to see if anything had happened to him. Emperor Hadrian was the same as always.

Mr. Night said, from somewhere behind me, "I can't understand how that wall fell down. It was a very solid wall."

We left the carrier pigeon at the base of the thicket behind Emperor Hadrian.

"How am I going to be able to communicate with Emperor Hadrian now?" I kept asking.

Mr. Night said: "Maybe you won't be able to reach him anymore ..."

I didn't want to accept a defeat like this, this terrible disaster in the night.

"No, Mr. Night, there must be some other way to do this ... Let's not despair from the start. The collapse of a wall and the death of a pigeon can't bury everything back in the darkness of past centuries all over again," I said.

Beside me, Mr. Night was pensive.

We had both sat down next to Emperor Hadrian's statue.

Orpheus' house was still in darkness.

From someplace behind us, the night beast howled.

I was gradually pulling myself together.

A light breeze from the sea began to blow over us.

"Mr. Night," I said. "I think we'll be able to show Emperor Hadrian the film *Last Tango in Paris* tomorrow night. If you can find a jeep as you told me you would in the hotel, we can quite easily carry a portable projector and the reels of the film here.

"Do you think the jeep will be able to get over the rocks?"

"I'll be able to use the jeep easily in the archaeological site, because I know the roads very well. Don't worry," he said.

The things that had been bothering both of us had just disappeared one by one.

"Can you see the Alpha Romeo, Mr. Night?" I asked my assistant.

He squinted his eyes and took a good look ahead into the darkness.

"The car's not there tonight," he said.

He had recovered as well.

Now he was more calm.

A little later we got up and bid farewell to Emperor Hadrian.

We started off towards the hotel.

When we got to the hotel, the sky was cloudy.

Orpheus

The sea was lively, waves were crashing and foaming on the shore. My assistant said: "Don't think about anything; get a good rest tonight. Tomorrow we're going to have a very unique evening!" We said goodbye.

I went inside and went up to my room.

For a long time I paced up and down in my room.

I couldn't sleep at all.

I was full of tension from what had happened.

I thought about Tunali Hilmi for a while.

That was an unbearable nightmare about Ankara!

As I thought over all these things, I fell into deep despair.

I was completely unsettled by the idea of being unable to communicate with Emperor Hadrian.

But everything I needed to show him the film *Last Tango in Paris* tomorrow night was ready.

I paced up and down in my room.

Suddenly I had an irresistible desire to write down for Emperor Hadrian all these things I had been thinking about.

This was more than a desire.

It was like a belief or a necessity.

With an irresistible urge, I took out my paper and began to write to Emperor Hadrian, knowing all the time that it would never reach him:

Dear Hadrian,

I'm having a terrible night.

The death of your carrier pigeon upset me very much. But I never want to accept that you are only a statue and I am only a person. That's why I want to write you this letter even though I have no hope that you will receive it.

Dear Hadrian, while I was in the newly developed city today, things that I neither know nor understand took place in the archaeological site.

And really, I can't figure out what's going on there anyway.

Tunali Hilmi, or Ankara, was as terrible as an explosion of consciousness that plastered so many photographs on top of one another.

As you heard, my assistant found the film reels and a projector.

Tomorrow night you will be able to see what you have been curious about for so long, a film.

It was like I was writing the letter to myself.

As I wrote, I was passing from belief to disbelief and back again.

For a while I thought of Orpheus' house there in its darkened state.

Maybe everything I had seen at the archaeological site last night was just some kind of coincidence.

It was as though a sentence had come all the way to my hotel room from far away and encircled my brain, as though it had united with the confusion in which I was living and was creating the vacuum into which I had fallen.

"… I was a person whose yesterday had been taken away and who had no tomorrow …"

Who had said this?

I lay down on my bed with the weariness imposed by this question. I drifted off.

The following morning, I woke up to a rapping on the door.

I quickly threw something on and opened the door.

It was the bellboy.

He was holding a letter with a seal on it. It was a letter from Emperor Hadrian.

Both the bellboy and I were quite surprised.

"Good morning, ma'am. I hope I didn't wake you.

"Your letter came very early. The carrier pigeon is different … A pure white, trembling pigeon brought this. It wouldn't eat the moistened bread I gave it. It's very nervous. I'm keeping it downstairs. Here's your letter," he said.

At that moment, I was so excited and happy that I didn't know what to do.

It had never occurred to me that Emperor Hadrian would send another pigeon!

Well, that's the Emperor.

He felt, saw, and understood everything!

I took the letter. I said to the bellboy, "Let me see this bird," as I went downstairs.

The pure white pigeon was cowering in a corner of the bellboy's room.

It was really a timid, nervous creature.

A platinum band was shining on its ankle.

Telling the bellboy to hold on to the bird, I went up to my room.

I looked closely at the seal on the letter.

Orpheus

It was Hadrian's seal.
I opened the letter with trembling hands.

Dear Eurydice,
If you ask me, you've made too much of the things that happened last night.
After all the things we've shared, the tension we experienced in the archaeological site last night increased with the mysterious death of the carrier pigeon and the apparently inexplicable collapse of the wall.
Dear Eurydice, belief and disbelief: that is my whole vision.
If I had to explain it in a different way, the part of me that is buried in the earth is disbelief, and the part of me that protrudes above the earth is belief.
And so you, as a result of the things you saw and experienced, came to notice me, and in fact found the border that has stood for years between my existence and your world.
Maybe you've crossed over it.
Dear Eurydice,
Orpheus and I have been sharing this ring of existence and vision for years.
By coming to know these things and by crossing over this border, you have created the third extension of an already existing bond. And you, by coming here, will either unravel this bond or become one more knot in it.
Do you remember, in order to console me in one of your letters, you wrote that most people can spend their whole lives always looking at the same things?
Well, now I'm agreeing that you're right.
By agreeing with you, I'm agreeing with all that you've lived, your world, this silent fate of mine, and that intangible border between us.
Dear Eurydice,
Surely the collapse of a wall and the death of a pigeon cannot end a communication such as this.
But I must say that writing this letter does not mean that the communication between us continued on perfectly.
Until now, you have always looked at Orpheus' house from my location. If you looked from Orpheus' house out to where I am, you would see that this eternal fate is not just limited to me.
Finally, you left the stone relief where it was and contented yourself with just knowing that it was there, and with looking at what kind of inscription it had and what kind of past it served.
Until now I have not spoken to you in my letters of my own age, of the confused triumph of my own times.

I haven't told you of the creative yet compliant drive of my slaves, of the free citizens wandering barefoot in the pure white temples built with marble I brought from all over the Empire, and of their striking creations.

And so, just as you haven't looked from Orpheus' house to where I am, you haven't looked from my age to where I am now, and perhaps you couldn't look that way.

You could only have looked out from a universe of ruins, where the joys of the magnificent days of a huge empire, desiccated by the drying winds of time, are jammed together in something called an "archaeological site."

And that's what happened, in fact.

Concerning that film you are going to show to me; I would like to look at the image that you call a film from these perspectives.

Emperor Hadrian

I was terrified as I read the letter from Emperor Hadrian.

The Emperor was taking Orpheus into his own universe and making me act as some kind of intermediary.

The connection he mentioned in his letter frightened me.

I tried to think of what could have caused Emperor Hadrian to write this complicated letter.

And strangely, his tone had shifted; he was mercilessly judging my point of view.

Starting again to pace up and down in my room, I tried to remember the first day Emperor Hadrian had sent me a letter …

He had found me!

He must know many things.

I wonder if the Orpheus he spoke of and the Orpheus I was after were in the same universe.

Yes, I think.

The letter I clutched in my hand could change the entire course of events.

I ripped up the letter I had left half-finished the night before and threw it away.

Then I began to write to the Emperor again:

Dear Hadrian,
I just read your letter twice.
One of the thinkers of my age, A.C., said: "Despite everything, I shall live."

Orpheus

He placed human fate on a scale and saw happiness as a spell, and as bravery.

The fact that being human is about dying was an outrage for him.

His shattering and upsetting writings shone with his love of the sea, the sky, and humanity.

A vagabond caught in a trap set by the absurdities of guilt and fate, a philosophy whose starting point is to commit suicide ... means that a man must have considered that his god might be deaf, that life is meaningless and the world unfair.

Dear Hadrian,

This is me!

A person who has revealed everything experiences a strange, gripping release. Right now, I feel that release.

A person must lose everything to gain everything.

These are my thoughts in answer to your letter. This is what I feel, and what I'm writing to you.

See you this evening.

Respectfully,
Eurydice

I put the letter in an envelope and went downstairs.

The white pigeon was next to the bellboy.

In order to put the letter on its ring, I bent down and reached out to it.

It was very frightened and flew over to the other side of the room.

The bellboy said: "It's very nervous, ma'am. I told you. It didn't eat a thing either."

With the letter in my hand, I went over to the other side of the room and tried to catch the bird.

It darted away again, to another corner.

Finally, the bellboy was able to grab it over by the door.

"Ma'am, if you only knew how its heart is beating. It's very afraid," he said.

I gently attached the letter to the ring on its claw.

I took the pigeon to the hotel door and let it go.

It traced a great arc in the air, then flew off towards the hilltop.

I spent the whole day in my room.

One by one, I reread all the letters I had received from Emperor Hadrian up to that point. At the same time, I had put on my bathing suit and was sunning myself on the towel I had spread on the balcony, drinking the iced Pepsi with lemon that I kept ordering.

The sun was very hot again.

Every once in a while, I darted into the coolness of my room and put a good coating of cream on my shoulders, knees, and face.

As I was sunbathing on the balcony, the Number II EGO bus passed by three or four times, each time completely empty.

I took my towel and went inside.

Just then someone knocked on the door.

"Come in," I said.

It was the bellboy.

"You have a phone call, ma'am," he said.

I put something on and went downstairs.

My assistant was talking to me in a happy mood from the other end.

"How are you? Everything's ready. I arranged for the jeep. I have the film reels. I'll pick you up at eight o'clock from the hotel. Are you ready?" he was asking.

"I'll get ready now. I sunbathed a little on the balcony today. I have interesting things to tell you. I got a very different letter from Emperor Hadrian today," I said.

On the other end of the line, my assistant was astonished.

"You got a letter? How did it come?" he asked.

"A white pigeon brought the letter. But if you ask me, what was really interesting was the content of the letter," I said.

Mr. Night was curious.

"Bring the letter with you, we'll read it on the way. I'll be in front of the hotel at exactly eight. See you," he said.

I hung up the phone and went up to my room.

There wasn't a whole lot of time before I would meet my assistant.

Since I was going to show the Emperor Hadrian *Last Tango in Paris* tonight, I dressed with care.

I combed my hair and arranged it differently. I put on my dark silk jumpsuit, got my cigarettes and matches, and went downstairs.

The last letter from Emperor Hadrian was in my bag.

Shortly after I came down, a jeep pulled up in front of the hotel.

Mr. Night had arrived.

I put out my cigarette and went outside.

I opened the door and sat down next to him.

Orpheus

Mr. Night was dressed differently than ever before.

He was even wearing a carnation on the lapel of his black jacket.

We were as excited as people who were going to the gala opening of a spectacular show.

Mr. Night stepped on the gas, and we began to move forward along the road beside the sea.

He was driving the jeep and talking to me at the same time.

"The projector and the film reels of *Last Tango in Paris* are in the back. I think it'll be very easy to set up the machine. I tried it once today.

"I keep thinking of something. On what do you plan to show the film?" he asked.

I suddenly thought of it.

"On the front of Orpheus' house," I said.

Mr. Night was intrigued: "On the front of Orpheus' house? What do you mean?" he asked.

"Very easy," I said. "We'll place the machine next to the statue of the Emperor Hadrian. The light will illuminate the facade of Orpheus' house."

My assistant was excited.

"What do you mean? You're going to use the front of Orpheus' house for a 'silver screen'?"

"Yes," I said.

The jeep kept climbing, driving around turns.

My assistant manoeuvred the jeep skillfully on those twisting, turning roads. A little while later we came to the archaeological site.

Mr. Night put the jeep into four-wheel drive and began to navigate among the centuries-old stones with unbelievable dexterity.

I saw the statue of Emperor Hadrian.

My assistant stopped the jeep twenty meters short of the statue.

"You told me about the letter the Emperor sent you," he said. "Do you have it with you?"

I pulled the letter out of my purse and gave it to Mr. Night.

He read the letter carefully from beginning to end by the light inside the jeep.

When he finished I asked, "What do you say?"

"You introduced a statue whose basic condition is loneliness to people and feelings. I was expecting something like this. Well, come along anyway," he said.

We got down together from the jeep and carried the tripod machine over by the statue.

Mr. Night set up the legs.

Over by the jeep, I was looking through the film reels.

My assistant came over to me and said in a voice Emperor Hadrian could not overhear: "I keep thinking about what he wrote in the letter. It was a very harsh letter. I wonder why? And I was thinking too: if we had completely excavated the statue and taken it out of the earth and put it in the museum, not one of the things it assumed in its letter would be valid. Isn't that so? Then, people would be taking its photograph," he said.

For a moment I thought of what Mr. Night had said.

Mr. Night took the projector out of the jeep and carried it over to place it in the tripod.

A light wind came up.

I looked at Orpheus' house.

It was completely dark.

Mr. Night put the projector in its place.

He went over and got the reels and placed them competently into the machine.

My eyes were on Orpheus' house.

Strangely, it seemed at one point that a light flashed on and then off.

I went behind the machine and started to adjust the focus.

Mr. Night had lit a cigarette and was watching me.

Somewhere behind us there was a rumble of thunder.

I was startled and moved over to the side.

Mr. Night said: "A storm is breaking."

I adjusted the focus again.

I pressed the start button.

Orpheus' house was lit up, completely white.

I played around with the reels. Some of them I wound, some got stuck.

At the same time I was looking at Orpheus' house in the white light.

We heard the thunder again. Lightning struck very near us. Large rain drops started to fall.

Mr. Night said: "See? It's starting to rain. The projector and the film reels will get wet."

I lifted my head and looked at the sky. The clouds had come down very low.

"It looks like it will rain harder, Mr. Night," I said. "Summer rain, it'll pass in a little while. Let's put the projector in the jeep right away."

It started raining harder.

My assistant and I got the film and the projector quickly into the jeep.

Then the two of us got in the front and sat.

A strong wind began to blow.

The raindrops drummed on the roof of the jeep and made puddles around it.

The windows had fogged over; it was impossible to see outside.

Every once in a while we could hear the sound of thunder coming from far away.

Mr. Night leaned down and turned on the jeep's radio.

He played with the station dial.

From the radio came a voice from the deep saying things, a broken sound I had never heard before, but that I somehow recognized as though from some explosion of consciousness.

... The tragedy of the Mediterranean comes from the sun, not from the mists like those of the north. Some evenings, above the sea, on the skirts of the mountains, night descends like a great, dark seamless folding, and then a great painful feeling of maturity rises from the still waters.

Where is that lofty balance of nature that comes with history, beauty, and goodness, that balance that even brings music to the innumerable bloody tragedies? We can't even think of it. We have turned our backs on nature, we are ashamed of beauty.

But nature is always there in front of us, and maintains its own silent skies and logic in spite of man's inanities.

The people of today believe that they must first save their bodies, and for this they are even willing to allow their souls to die for a bit, but can a soul die for just a short time?

Civilizations cannot be established by giving somebody or other a slap. Civilizations are founded by pain and courage, by the clash of ideas, the bleeding of thought.

The world that I and others like me want is not one in which people do not kill one another, but a world in which it would be unjustifiable to kill someone.

In this we are in contradiction. Because the world we live in is one where it is considered just to kill. If one wants to change this, it seems necessary to bear in mind that one might have to kill.

Mr. Night and I were astonished at what we heard.

"Who was that speaking?" he asked.

"It's a strange thing; it's like I know him, know him very well, but I just can't place him," I said.

The rain had let up.

We got out of the jeep.

Walking on the earth moistened by the rain, I went over to Emperor Hadrian's statue.

Behind me, Mr. Night was carrying the tripod. After he placed it where it had been a little before, he went and got the projector, brought it over, and set it up. He attached the reels and gave them quite a professional spin.

He lit a cigarette and went over to the statue.

The rain and the clouds had really broken up and disappeared.

My eyes were on Orpheus' house.

The house was dark.

I focused the projector again. I gave the reel a turn and pressed the button.

Orpheus' house was illuminated, completely white.

"Dear Hadrian, this is the silver screen!

"Here's *Last Tango in Paris*," I said.

The images of the film passed through the light.

"… They call this the cinema," said Tom. "This is my crew, and we're making a film." He pressed his lips lightly against Jeanne's. His actions were no different from those of a naughty child.

"If I kiss you that could be a film."

Tom stroked Jeanne's hair.

"If I stroke your hair that could be a film."

Tom lost control of himself and even started to dance in front of the camera. Jeanne tried to stop him.

"Enough, stop them," she said, waving both arms and trying to drive the cameraman away.

"I told you, they're my crew. It's a new …"

"The film is wound wrong," shouted Mr. Night. "Emperor Hadrian is going to mix up everything on the screen! We must have mixed up the reels."

And so we had.

I lifted up the handle and cut off the film.

I turned to Mr. Night: "You're right," I said. "I was in a hurry. The reels got mixed up."

"There's not much time until dawn," said Mr. Night. "I don't think we're going to be able to fix this tonight. We have to rewind all the reels."

I turned around and looked at Emperor Hadrian.

As always, he was just staring straight ahead.

Suddenly, in the white light on the front of Orpheus' house, a curtain opened.

It was such a completely unexpected thing for me that I just froze.

The curtain closed.

"Did you see that, Mr. Night?" I asked.

He had seen it.

He was excited too.

"A curtain was opened and closed," he said.

My eyes were on the white light on Orpheus' house.

There was no movement.

I lowered the handle of the machine again.

Strangely, this time a different section of the film *Last Tango in Paris* began to play.

The sunbeams were playing on the intricate iron fence work on the bridge. Without their knowledge even, they were trapped within the flowered iron columns.

They did not know one another. The woman was the age of his daughter. The broad-brimmed brown hat on her bent head was pushed down a little. Young and beautiful, she moved in a way that could almost be called provocative. As she swung the bag that she carried on its long straps, the wind blew her jet-black hair over her white fur coat. Her full lips were moist and fresh. The grey knit dress wrapping her well-developed body displayed her walk, and her long legs captured the rhythmic movements of her fur coat.

The lines of the man's face resembled those of a hawk. Hard, rigid, and mocking.

Every now and then he ran his hands through his hair, then put them in the pockets of his camel-hair coat. He looked like an American gangster in the soiled but well-made coat.

Their names were Paul and Jeanne.

Two people walking along the promenade.

I lifted the arm of the projector.

The images suddenly disappeared.

Mr. Night asked: "Did something happen? Why did you stop the film?"

"Look closely. The curtain at the window opened and closed again. It's as though Orpheus is becoming part of the film.

"That's why I stopped the film. But when I turned off the film, the curtain closed again," I said.

Mr. Night said: "Believe me, I didn't see anything; I must have been absorbed in the film. From now on I'll look for that too."

I lowered the arm on the machine again.

The film continued.

Paul suddenly embraces Jeanne. He pulls her down by the base of the wall next to the window. He puts his hand inside her thick coat by the collar and embraces her. Paul pulls Jeanne to him and starts to fondle her through her dress. Then with a sudden movement, he opens the buttons of her dress. They start to take off one another's clothes. Their breathing grows more rapid. Paul kisses Jeanne's breasts. He bends down ...

The film suddenly broke.

I turned to Mr. Night angrily.

"We have such an old copy here, it looks like it's going to keep breaking," I said.

I was annoyed because we couldn't show the film properly.

We pulled the reels off and started to work on them in the starlight.

As we tried to fix this old copy of *Last Tango in Paris*, the night animal kept howling.

I turned and looked at Orpheus' house. There wasn't the slightest movement in the white light on the facade.

I lowered the handle.

The band of film hit the light.

Orpheus

The film came alive again.

Paul brings his two hands to Jeanne's face and begins to stroke her. Then his hands move down to Jeanne's neck and shoulders. They move a little closer to one another. Paul begins to kiss Jeanne's hair.

The man doing the sound recording has knelt down and, with an earset on, is waving his microphone to the left and right, recording the sound of the animals nearby.

"Excuse me, Hadrian, sir!" I shouted.

I raised the arm of the machine.

"Forgive me, Emperor, sir, they've cut the film up and turned it into nonsense. You saw how it suddenly jumped from place to place! And besides, as I told you already, this is an old scratchy copy," I said.

The Emperor Hadrian's stone face was looking ahead as usual.

The night animal howled somewhere behind me.

I looked at Orpheus' house.

It was pure white.

Next to me, Mr. Night said: "Soon it will be morning. In the daylight, all the images will disappear. If you'd like, we could turn the reels and show the end of the film."

There was nothing I could do.

I began to turn the reels.

Then I lowered the handle.

The whiteness on Orpheus' house took color and came alive again.

Jeanne finds her key in her bag. Then, after a long struggle, she opens the door.

Paul is right behind her.

He pushes the door with his shoulder.

Jeanne, inside the house, begins to run forward.

I began to see incredible things.

Across from me, a third person appeared along with the two who were chasing one another in the film.

This person was out of place, caught in a whirlpool of images, someone who didn't know what to do.

I recognized him.

Paul shouts after Jeanne. He says, "Since we've come this far, we can't turn back now."

Orpheus was trying to get out of the light.

I was trying to see his face.

Along with such a vast distance, what kind of past was it that was struggling like this in front of me? What kind of future?

Or, what kind of distance was it in whose pincers we were struggling so hard that we took refuge in the trap of a fight that was so close by?

This was the proof of everything.

I had to look at him.

I had to look at him as though I was looking at a trap.

I had to look at the whole map of judgment on the lines of his face, the map that would stop all the decaying, destroying answers to problems, stop fate itself, the map that was set up to make a new fate.

And there it was!

In spite of everything, I had seen him.

But did he see me?

Did he have to?

Or, did he have to look in order to see me?

Belief. It had entrapped me again.

It had caught me tightly once again, like the writing of a dream of fate with its magic letters.

I could only look at him once.

It was just like the disappearance of an omen, like the loss of an expired memory.

This pitch-black house was so powerful it could destroy the mysterious stillness that suffused the stones of the archaeological site whenever I came, and this destruction coincided with the penumbra of an eternal dawn …

Was this really possible?

Or had I really come here?

Paul is now shouting, "This girl is mine," and going on. "You ran away from me but no matter where you went in the world, I would have found you. So I found you in the end. Because …"

Orpheus

Jeanne opens the drawer. She takes out the gun she had inherited from her father. The cold piece of iron in her hand is heavy and powerful.

I was trying to cut the film.
The arm of the machine was locked.
The film was continuing.
Despite exerting all my strength, I couldn't move the arm from its place.

Paul takes a step closer to Jeanne. He doesn't even notice that the girl's coat has opened.
She turns the gun barrel towards Paul.

Orpheus made a movement to come towards me.

… The girl pulls the trigger …

Orpheus staggered, turning where he stood, and leaned against the window.
The door opening onto the balcony, unable to hold this weight, opened completely.
Orpheus' hair was caught in the morning breeze.
"Come on, let's go," said Mr. Night.

December 15, 1982
Ankara

Lightning Source UK Ltd.
Milton Keynes UK
UKHW012246280822
407869UK00010B/183